The Unfinished Painting

THE UNFINISHED PAINTING

Mercedes Aguirre

Translated from Spanish by Richard Buxton

The Book Guild Ltd

First published in Great Britain in 2020 by
The Book Guild Ltd
9 Priory Business Park
Wistow Road, Kibworth
Leicestershire, LE8 0RX
Freephone: 0800 999 2982
www.bookguild.co.uk
Email: info@bookguild.co.uk
Twitter: @bookguild

Copyright © 2020 Mercedes Aguirre
Original title in Spanish: El cuadro inacabado. Madrid, Eride Ediciones 2013.

The right of Mercedes Aguirre to be identified as the author of this
work has been asserted by her in accordance with the
Copyright, Design and Patents Act 1988.

Translated by Richard Buxton

All rights reserved. No part of this publication may be
reproduced, transmitted, or stored in a retrieval system, in any form or by any means,
without permission in writing from the publisher, nor be otherwise circulated in
any form of binding or cover other than that in which it is published and without
a similar condition being imposed on the subsequent purchaser.

Typeset in 11pt Baskerville

Printed and bound by CPI Group (UK) Ltd, Croydon, CR0 4YY

ISBN 978 1913208 745

British Library Cataloguing in Publication Data.
A catalogue record for this book is available from the British Library.

The characters and plot of this novel are wholly fictitious. However, the nineteenth-century historical background is real, as are the Pre-Raphaelite painters whom I mention, as well as other persons from the same historical era in England. I have tried to adapt my central character to the period which I aim to recreate, situating him in a context which might have been authentic.

An unknown location

The present day

WHAT MAKES US ADMIRE A PAINTING? SOMETIMES THE beauty of its shapes, the composition, the colour. Sometimes the subject, real or symbolic. But sometimes what stirs us is an intangible, indescribable quality which throws our state of mind into turmoil. The painter Edward Burne-Jones once said that a picture is a beautiful, romantic dream of something that never was and never will be, in a light better than any light that ever shone, in a land no one can define or remember, only desire.

It was conceived as an oil painting, in vivid colours. The figures, still indistinct, mingled in a jumbled whole, the outlines of faces and contours of bodies ill-defined. They were realised with rapid brushstrokes here and there, incomplete lines straight or curved, sharper or as yet formless. In the far distance, what looked like the sky stood out with exquisite blue tones. It was, you could say, a vision that had emerged from a dream.

It lay in a corner, almost hidden; there wasn't enough light to appreciate it. But then just the same was true of all the other paintings piled up haphazardly in that room. Time had smothered them in dust, dulling their former brilliance.

In all the months and years which had passed, no one had claimed it or found a home for it in a museum, alongside great works of art. There it was, waiting for someone to recognise its existence.

Ely, Cambridgeshire

October 1858

1

An icy gust greeted Alexander as he stepped off the train in the little station which was his destination. At last there would be no more of the discomforts of a journey that was quite unfamiliar to him. The noise and smoke of the huge steam engine had accompanied him throughout the long and tiring trip which had begun in London very early that morning.

A few minutes before they came into the station, the silhouette of the cathedral's distant grey towers informed him that they were nearing his home, the small town of Ely, not far from Cambridge.

He gave his address to the coachman who was waiting for him and who helped him with his luggage: a trunk, a small suitcase and two carelessly wrapped packages tied up with string.

Everything seemed so different to him, as if, instead of an absence of just two years, he had left home far longer ago, and could remember neither the route nor the landscape.

Gradually, though, his memory was reawakening. He recognised the canal, with its still waters almost frozen over, as a line of ducks glided idly past. On the other side, green hills; in the distance, the great cathedral. He gazed up at it, recalling how often he had drawn each arch and capital, painstakingly reflecting their every detail on paper. He had spent hours sitting in the park opposite, trying to reproduce the sharp outline of the towers against the light of the setting sun, the colours of stone against the colours of the sky.

Now, as he passed by once again, he caught sight of the glorious stained glass of the façade. How he had admired the artist who had transformed coloured glass into human figures, who sprang into life with each ray of sunlight!

When he opened the door of the house he had lived in for most of his life, the smell which greeted him was close and fusty. The furniture, the carpets, the creaking floor, all these brought back a host of memories: his mother, always serious and seemingly absent, embroidering in the living room; his father reading the newspaper in his favourite armchair…

But that was long ago. Both had died when he was little more than a child, before he had time to upset them by dedicating himself to art, instead of working in the family shop as his elder brother had done. His parents, he well knew, would have spent months reproaching him. It wasn't that he was unwilling to do what was expected of him and so honour their memory. It was just that his vocation outweighed any other emotion. Painting *had* to be his profession. An uncertain one, perhaps; but it would entirely fulfil his longings. It was what he had been born for. So one day, two years ago, he had adventurously decided to move to London, in search of a way of learning, of improving his technique, of turning himself into an artist.

Alexander carefully hung his overcoat and hat on the stand, and made sure that the trunk, suitcase and packages were safely stored at the entrance. Then he walked through the whole house to check what state it was in. Everything seemed in order. Presumably Mrs Smith had organised the cleaning as efficiently and regularly as she had done when he used to live there.

The staircase grumbled as he trod on it, as if it had grown used to being unsullied, and was protesting at the sudden weight of a man.

The upstairs bedrooms were exactly as he had left them; in fact nothing had changed for years. In what had been his parents' room there was the same bed of dark wood with its red bedspread, the same flowered curtains at the window. Alexander hadn't dared move a single one of the objects from where his mother had placed them, as if she were still sitting at her dressing table, brushing the ringlets of her long hair.

In Alexander's mind the years merged.

He left till last the room which filled him with the keenest anticipation: his studio, the small, intimate, ground-floor room where he had spent so many hours thinking, mixing colours, gazing, painting.

Faces looked out at him from canvases hanging on the walls, or still resting on easels. He recognised the half-closed eyes and gentle smile of the peasant girl with her basket of apples, and the superior expression of the young woman doing embroidery. They seemed to be greeting him, happy to see their creator again. He recognised too the features of the village girl who had modelled for many of them, posing for him with infinite patience.

Yet he smiled to himself as he realised how much his style had developed. His brushwork was stronger and firmer now, his use of colour more assured. The works in front of him were not his own, but those of another artist. From London he had brought paintings he had produced there: some watercolours, two oils, as well as several drawings which could serve as sketches for the future. In all of them he could see how he had progressed beyond the art he had made before.

He turned and closed the door. Putting all this in order would take hours.

He made a cup of tea and took it into the small living room. The damp and the cold had made him shiver, and he needed to warm up before starting to arrange his things. It had already grown dark, and he hadn't enough oil to keep the lamp lit for much longer.

The tea revived some of his lost energy. He felt ready to take a new step in his life, one which, with luck, might lead to personal satisfaction and professional success. At his present age of twenty-three, his teachers in the Working Men's College in London had already managed to arouse the admiration of experts in the art world. And he himself had enough ambition to drive him on his journey.

2

He had spent an uneasy night. The enveloping silence had been more disturbing than the shrillest of noises. He had grown used to the constant clamour of the London streets: carriages on cobblestones, horses' hooves, the voices of passers-by, rain beating on his window…

Memories of London had also kept him awake: the house he had lived in, his friends, his work, that almost obsessive desire to learn, to draw out the most he could from the teaching he was receiving. From the first day he had been astonished by the achievements of the other artists, yet also a little in awe of them. It was true that his teachers' paintings had received every kind of criticism, some of it harsh; but aren't the greatest artists precisely those for whom acceptance by their contemporaries comes slowest? There could be no doubt about the true genius of the group of painters who had formed what they called the Brotherhood.

Alexander felt proud to have had at least a small share in their experiences.

But now it was time for *his* journey.

And here was another anxiety which had gripped him: the impatience to begin that new painting which for now existed only in his mind, but which was struggling to force its way out, to take shape and come to life.

At one point in the long night he lit a candle and took up the book which he had left on the table, poems signed by his friend and master Dante Gabriel Rossetti.

He read a few sonnets and felt better – nearer to the man he might never see again, but whose spirit would remain close to him always. There are bonds which distance cannot break.

They had much in common. They had laughed and sketched together, chatting and arguing about art for hours. But Gabriel's creativity knew no limits. Not satisfied with painting, he had also tried to reflect his intense emotions in writing, with the most wonderful verses. They were dedicated to the women he loved or the characters who fascinated him, drawn from the pages of the greatest literary works, from myths or legends, or from everyday life. Into everything he poured the intense passion which was his trademark.

When day came and light began to filter through the curtains, Alexander woke from a shallow sleep and set about beginning this first day of a new life in his home town.

As he had supposed, it took him several hours to put his belongings in order: the clothes in his trunk, his books and all the paraphernalia from his stay in London. But domestic chores didn't matter that much to him. His main interest lay in the still pristine canvases, the brushes, the tubes of colour. There too were the notes he had taken in the art classes – a little treasure, those pages filled with the comments and criticisms of another of his masters, John Ruskin, whose repute was swiftly spreading through London's intelligentsia.

When he had finished dressing and had hung his suits in the bedroom wardrobe, he decided that sometime he would have to go into the village. There were people to contact, provisions and other necessaries to buy from the market. His financial situation depended mainly on what he had inherited from his father, a shopkeeper belonging to the growing middle class; though there was also the money he had made in London. Enough to pay a couple of servants to run the house, maybe also a boy to look after the small garden.

In spite of his resolve to dedicate himself entirely to his work, he knew he couldn't become a recluse and withdraw completely from the world. There were neighbours and friends who valued and respected him; they would surely be glad to see him again. Maybe one day he could invite people to take tea. A bit of social life would do him no harm.

Outside it was raining. The lanes round the house had filled with mud. Two boys were loading wood onto a cart; in the house opposite, the curtains moved slightly as Alexander began his walk, half-hidden by an umbrella.

Nothing had changed: he realised it at last. But why *should* it have changed? It had been only two years, and in a small place like Ely life edged forward in a monotone, without variations or surprises. Since the recent works to construct the canal and the new railway station, nothing much had happened. It wasn't like London: here there was no sign of the industrial developments which were altering the landscape throughout the country.

He recognised 'The Lamb' at once, the little hotel in the High Street where his father used to go to meet his friends. A good place to call in for a hot soup, he thought.

'Mr Knight! What a surprise!'

'How long it's been since we saw you here!'

Alexander responded with a smile to the intrigued questions of the two men sitting next to the fireplace. The brief conversation, about nothing in particular, made him feel he was among friends again.

These people knew him, had known his family before him, and were going to play a part in his life once again. And in a small, essentially rural community, Alexander might soon become a celebrity. Hadn't he been rubbing shoulders with the leading artists of the day? Joining in London's fashionable circles? Socialising with painters and poets? Even if those particular painters and poets had broken with mainstream British tradition, arousing equally attraction and repulsion.

3

IN THE DAYS WHICH FOLLOWED, ALEXANDER PLUNGED into frantic activity. Domestic affairs were regulated thanks to Mrs Smith and her niece, a girl of barely fifteen already used to being in service with well-to-do families in the village. When she looked at Mr Knight, very young though he yet was, she saw the complete gentleman. Maybe a bit eccentric, but after all he was an artist, wasn't he? And certainly good-looking, with his thick dark hair, big blue eyes and those soft features set in a round, boyish face. His fingers were long and slender. When he held a paintbrush, they seemed to be caressing it.

Alexander had prepared his studio so as to start work at the earliest possible moment. He had set the old canvases to one side in readiness for creating something quite new, adapting the manner of his masters to his own personal style.

In London he had already tried to reproduce the themes which fascinated the men who called themselves the Pre-Raphaelite Brotherhood. It was a name they themselves had invented because, they maintained, they drew their inspiration from the painters before Raphael, convinced that that was where true art was to be found. Arthurian legends, religious stories drawn from the Bible, literary or classical characters and motifs, these were their themes. What a miracle, that Ophelia floating among the flowers, exhibited at the Royal Academy by John Everett Millais, Gabriel's good friend! What an overwhelming success, that of Rossetti's most recent work!

To find out more about the gods and heroes of antiquity, Alexander had often visited the British Museum, enraptured by the sculptures recently transported from the Athenian Acropolis, Pheidias's tremendous creations. Such beauty in their curves, in their perfect delicacy of form.

He had read the myths, those sometimes-terrible stories in which the most contradictory emotions intermingled: the most selfless love, the most appalling hatred. And he had decided that this would be the theme of his next painting: a myth. Not just any myth, but the myth which united the goddess of love with a sweet and tender mortal youth, whose beauty had the power to arouse the passion of the goddesses of Olympus. The goddess was called Venus; the youth, Adonis. It was a tale which had a dramatic climax, but which already at the outset held within it the seed of disaster. This is what Alexander had read, over and over again, in one of his books:

There once was a king whose daughter, Myrrha, one day conceived a passion for her own father. So violent was the desire that invaded her that it threatened to consume her. So one night, in the darkness, she secretly crept into the king's bed. Not recognising his own daughter, he allowed himself to give way to the longing which overcame him to hold in his arms the body of a beautiful woman. When the same thing had happened for several nights, the king wanted to know who the unknown woman was who had given herself to him each night, and whose face he had never seen. So one night he decided to light a lamp – and discovered the dreadful truth of the woman's identity. Myrrha fled, for she too was ashamed of what she had done. But the gods, instead of punishing her for her perverted desires, turned her into the tree which would bear her name: myrrh. And eventually from her – or from the tree – was born the most beautiful baby boy imaginable, a boy who grew up to be jealously fought over by the goddesses who yearned for him. In the end it was Venus, goddess of beauty, who triumphed. Adonis stayed by her side. What tenderness between them, what caresses. Two perfect beings, together forever. But though myths resemble fairy tales in some ways, they rarely have a happy ending. One day, when Adonis went hunting in the mountains, he was savaged by a boar and died of his wounds. Venus's pain was beyond description. But what could she do? To bring him back to life was impossible. But what she could do was to mourn for him for all eternity, and to leave behind a permanent memory of his existence: a flower with red petals, stained with the colour of his blood.

Alexander was already beginning to imagine the beauty of the two lovers: the goddess and the youth. And Myrrha too, the woman who had been the boy's mother; though transformed into a suffering tree, she yet retained within her something of her human nature, and her forbidden passion. And Cinyras, the king, guilty without his knowledge of a wicked act – a model of human weakness.

He uncovered the canvas which stood ready on the easel, and prepared to paint.

Cambridge

The present day

1

THAT EVENING SHE HAD LEFT THE LIBRARY A BIT earlier than usual. She had collected her rucksack from the locker and walked down the street, not bothering about the rain which had been falling all day.

She had been working for hours, satisfied that she had nearly completed another chapter of her thesis. But suddenly she felt unable to continue. The books she had been consulting seemed meaningless; she decided to put them back on the shelves.

As if borne along by some *idée fixe*, she dashed out of the building, only to realise she had no notion of why she had done it. And now she was going to waste time that she could have made good use of. She hadn't arranged to meet anyone later, and had no plans for the evening. Her boyfriend Paul had gone to football training. She usually enjoyed his company, but this time she was glad to have a few hours to herself, to work on the doctoral thesis which was now well advanced.

Barely conscious of where she was going, Emma suddenly found herself in front of the railings of the Fitzwilliam Museum. Without a moment's hesitation she made for the entrance, walking past the white columns which, in the manner of a classical temple, supported a pediment ornamented with reliefs.

She knew every room, every corner intimately. Since starting her course in the History of Art at the University of Cambridge she had spent a good deal of time there, fascinated by the collection: in the basement, the Greek and Roman antiquities; on the first floor, after you walked from the hall up the wonderful marble staircase, examples of English painting along with works of the Italian Renaissance and the Impressionists. She had studied her favourites meticulously, sitting in front of them, notebook in hand, preparing a presentation for the next tutorial. Of course she knew of other museums more celebrated than the Fitzwilliam. She had been several times to the National Gallery and the Tate, once too to the Manchester Museum; all housed incomparable collections. But the Fitzwilliam was special to her. There was something antique about its style, something that transported you to another age. She knew it had been founded in 1845 thanks to donations by the Viscount Fitzwilliam who lent it his name, and whose own artworks and books had passed to it. In the years that followed, till the present day, more gifts and acquisitions had enriched it, creating its current prosperous situation, a site of exhibitions, conferences and other events. And entry was free – another reason to keep going back.

Well, she thought, since she had nothing better to do, time spent in the museum was always productive.

It was almost empty. Soon it would be closing time; the usual groups of tourists had already left.

She went directly to the room with the nineteenth-century paintings. These were the works which interested her most, and which formed the subject of her research.

After nearly two years of intensive work, she knew the lives of these artists as well as she knew her own family. She had a passion for entering their world – alien and distant in time, yet at the same time very close – to unearth the tiniest secrets which could explain why, how and when these paintings had been created.

She walked restlessly from one side of the room to the other. The museum had always offered her an agreeable sensation of tranquillity. Even in the period before her exams those galleries had been her refuge. But this time she felt uncomfortable; and she couldn't explain why. What exactly was she doing there *now*? She would scarcely have time to do any work before they closed…

Had she gone there for some specific reason, and then forgotten it?

Emma couldn't say.

And when she saw one of the custodians coming towards her, she realised they were about to shut.

'Excuse me, miss. Visiting time's over.'

'Sorry,' Emma replied quickly. 'Don't worry. I'm off.'

As she headed towards the exit, she was aware of the presence of a man behind her. She hadn't noticed him before, but apparently he was coming from the same room where she had been a few minutes earlier. He had fair hair and walked with a slight stoop, as if he were too tall and had the habit of bending down to the height of those around him.

She watched him go down the street in the opposite direction to the one she had to take.

Suddenly Emma felt tired, more tired than she usually felt after a day's work. Maybe she was catching the flu.

Trying to forget what had happened in the last hour, she arrived back at the flat where she lived, a flat shared with a group of other young people, all postgraduates like her.

Mary was already there. Brown-haired and plump, lively and cheerful, she was doing a thesis on psychology. She was curled up on the dilapidated living room sofa, with a glass of wine in one hand and a mobile in the other. She seemed in a state of utterly peaceful communion with herself.

'It's time you put in an appearance,' she commented as she saw Emma walk in, with a hint of reproach in her voice. 'I was texting you to see whether I was supposed to stay here all evening drinking on my own. But now I see that…'

'Sorry I didn't ring,' said Emma. 'I finished hours ago in the library, but… I don't know… I've felt a bit strange this evening.'

Mary laughed and changed her posture, stretching her legs and resting them on the little table in front of her, wobbling the bottle of red wine which stood on some papers.

Emma took off her jacket and flopped down on the sofa next to her friend. 'And how are you?'

'Crappy. In the department they had me checking the timetable and I couldn't get a single page written. I've been waiting all day to see if that cretin Justin would deign to go out with me. I think I badly need a man in my bed…'

Mary's real name was María Castilla. By origin she was Spanish: her father was from Extremadura, though her mother was English. She had been born in Madrid and spent the first years of her life there. But she had become so integrated into the British way of life that she couldn't say she felt particularly Spanish, even if sometimes her character revealed her roots.

Emma and Mary had been good friends for a number of years since they first met in Cambridge, both slightly lost but still glad to be embarking on a new stage of their lives as university students. While Emma had opted for History of Art, Mary had read Psychology. Now she was working part-time in the same department where she had begun her studies.

Gradually Emma began to feel better, soothed by Mary's incessant chatter. But suddenly she remembered the man she had seen in the museum. She had the impression that there was something familiar about him, that she had seen him somewhere before.

It was odd: nothing that had happened to her that evening seemed explicable.

2

SHE WOKE WITH A START IN THE MIDDLE OF THE night. She'd heard Mary switching the television on and off, and her other flatmate Alice returning from the pub where she worked. She'd also heard Justin, the music student who had the room at the end of the corridor. He lived in his own world practising the violin, and didn't mind at all being the only man living with a group of women. But it wasn't the noises made by the others which had woken Emma, but something like a nightmare, which had left her with a strange feeling of dread.

She had dreamed of the Fitzwilliam Museum. It looked more or less as it had done the previous evening, except that now it had the appearance of a different era, more than a hundred years before the present. Emma herself was there, watching some people carrying a painting, presumably to be placed in one of the galleries. She couldn't see the painting itself, but she could make out three letters: they might have been "A. R. K.", though she couldn't be absolutely sure. At one moment in the dream she saw some men talking among themselves, and felt the urge to communicate with them. But try as she might her voice didn't carry, or they didn't understand her, even though she felt that what she had to tell them was important.

Emma couldn't get back to sleep. For some reason those images, which had seemed so real, had left her uneasy. Usually she slept well, tired out after a day studying or a night partying with friends. Sometimes she stayed at Paul's house, where she always slept deeply and peacefully.

Paul. Suddenly she remembered him. She hadn't called him. She hoped he wouldn't be upset.

They'd been going out together for a few months, and everything seemed to be going well. He was an affectionate young man who had just finished a Master's in Law; he worked part-time in an insurance company. He also played football for one of the university teams. You could say he was good-looking, with an athlete's body, very short fair hair and a sexy smile which Emma adored. And she couldn't resist his charm, the way he caressed her and kissed her when they were alone in his room. Maybe things had moved a bit too quickly, but she didn't mind. Paul filled a void in her life, and supplied the warmth which she always thought she lacked. She wasn't quite sure whether what she felt for him was really love, and she was afraid of commitment; but for now this was what she needed.

Suddenly her memory of him became more intense. Alone in her bed, Emma longed for those moments of extreme pleasure, followed by the touch of his back when they slept after making love, their bodies pressed very close together.

*

When she got up it was already gone eight. She showered, then dressed quickly in jeans and the jumper she had just bought in the sales. She knew Mary was in the kitchen; she had heard the noise of washing up.

'Morning.' She was conscious that her voice was shaky, as if it needed an effort to speak.

'You look terrible,' was Mary's reaction. 'What's wrong? I thought I was the one with a hangover, but I must look better than you do.' Mary was wearing a top with coloured patterns. She obviously enjoyed attracting attention.

'I didn't sleep well. I don't know, maybe I'm not so well…'

Emma poured herself some tea from the pot which Mary had just made. There weren't many clean plates, so she put a slice of toast on a paper serviette.

'You work too hard, and that's not good. All those nineteenth-century characters of yours are half-demented; maybe it's catching.'

As she sipped her tea, Emma was pensive. The museum. She just had to go back.

What she expected to find there, she had no notion. If she'd been able to think clearly, she would have realised that her best plan was to spend the morning in the library, adding more facts to the chapter she was working on. But a single idea boiled in her mind, and she couldn't get rid of it. The only way to relieve her anxiety was to go to the museum.

Mary gave her a strange look but said nothing. Though she and Emma got on well, they had very different temperaments. Sometimes Mary mocked Emma's serious and transcendental air – not maliciously, simply trying to liven her up, in search of something they could laugh at together. Maybe studying psychology had turned Mary into a woman with fewer inhibitions, an optimist, or sometimes rather a cynic. Emma was always surprised to see her so relaxed, as if nothing mattered to her, with her striking and almost adolescent appearance. But as a student she was conscientious, responsible, full of projects for the future and always ready to offer help if someone needed it.

Emma arrived at the museum almost automatically, as if compelled by an external force; she was oblivious of the traffic noise around her, the passing cyclists, the groups of students on their way to lectures. It was sunny, and mild for October, but she didn't notice that either.

At this time in the morning the museum was busier than the previous evening. There were Japanese tourists, more students and a group of children in school uniform; their teacher was trying and failing to keep them quiet.

Emma headed once more for the room at the end of the first floor and sat in front of the pictures. What was she expecting to find in them? Did she think she would recognise the painting she had dreamed about?

In front of her was the collection of nineteenth-century works. The oils on the wall, some larger, some smaller, lay next to magnificently preserved ceramics and cabinets.

She lost all sense of time, sitting motionless and gazing absently. But suddenly she noticed that the people around her were no longer the same ones as before. The children and tourists had disappeared, to be replaced by another set of characters who paraded strangely in front of her eyes, as if they belonged to another era. You could tell this from their clothes: men dressed in dark colours and wearing top hats, a woman with a long dress and wide green skirt…

Emma shook her head in a state of shock. She must have dozed off. But how could that be? She didn't remember having closed her eyes…

A moment later, the room recovered its former appearance: the same girl in black trousers and red jacket, an older man in a raincoat, the children in their uniforms.

Emma began to get seriously worried. Ever since the previous afternoon, inexplicable things seemed to have been happening to her. And then there was last night's dream. Obviously, dreams can be strange without there being a reason for it; but *this* dream seemed to be connected with everything else. Maybe Mary was right, that it was all a result of her exhaustion, those endless hours spent in intensive work on finishing her thesis.

She looked again at the paintings, captivated as usual by their beauty. Those landscapes of the English coast with their soft colours; the girl with the long, thick, wavy hair painted by John Everett Millais; the portraits; above all, Burne-Jones's two angels playing harps.

She couldn't say how long she'd been in the museum. It might have been two hours or ten minutes. And she still couldn't properly explain her presence there, even if to enjoy walking around the collection was something quite normal for her.

It was when she was already about to leave that she saw him in the distance. He had his back to her, but she still recognised him. The same man as the day before, tall and slim, with straight fair hair. From far off he looked young, even a student like her, yet from what she had seen of him before, she could have sworn he was in his forties.

If you thought about it, it wasn't so unusual for the same person to keep coming back to the museum. Perhaps, like her, he was doing research. Or perhaps he had nothing better to do than spend his time looking at art.

She went out into the street in terror, her heart pounding, filled with inexplicable anxiety.

She had to call Paul. She wanted to see Paul.

Would he be angry with her?

An hour later they met in a café. On the other side of the street was the main door of King's College, the gateway to the lawns, the students' accommodation and the Chapel, that magnificent Gothic icon of the city of Cambridge.

Paul wasn't angry: quite the opposite. He looked overjoyed to see her again – you might imagine that he'd forgotten that she'd broken her promise to ring him the previous day. But he soon realised there was something the matter with her. That frightened look, that desperate expression…

'Tell me what's wrong. Don't you feel well?' He reached over the table and squeezed her hand. His touch seemed to reassure her.

'The truth is, I don't know,' replied Emma, trying to force a smile. 'It's hard to explain. Maybe you'll think I'm a bit stupid.'

'Come on!' He laughed. 'That's one thing I'd never think of *you*!'

Emma told him as best she could about her weird impressions of the previous evening, including her dream and the sensation of being in another time. As she related all this she was aware of not sounding very credible.

But Paul looked at her seriously. 'Are you sure you didn't have too much to drink last night? Did you smoke something funny with one of these friends of yours?'

Emma shook her head. 'Of course I'm sure. I just went to bed; I didn't drink or smoke or take anything. You know me well enough: you know I don't enjoy those sorts of things.'

'Maybe you should have an aspirin and rest in bed. You're working hard, and you might be getting a cold.'

Just what Mary had thought. It was the most reasonable explanation. Nothing to worry about.

The two of them continued to drink their coffee in silence, ignoring the constant comings and goings in the café.

'Come to mine,' said Paul at last, taking her hand again. 'This evening I'll be free. I'll make us something to eat and we can listen to music and unwind.'

3

EVERY MORNING EMMA WENT BACK TO THE MUSEUM. And every night she dreamed about that mysterious painting, and about unknown characters who, without a doubt, belonged to the past. Being with Paul made no difference to a situation which kept inexplicably repeating itself. He'd done his best to look after her in his own flat, making her feel at ease and desired. They had had dinner together, made love, and shared domestic chores such as cleaning and shopping. But it was no use. Emma's condition hadn't improved.

It wasn't that she was ill. In other respects she was well: she had a good appetite and enough energy to lead a completely normal life. Unlike some other girls of her age Emma was concerned about her health and her fitness: she avoided too much alcohol, followed an almost vegetarian diet and went regularly to a gym. Whatever was happening to her now had nothing to do with her body, but with her mind. That peculiar obsession with the museum, and the dream-visions she had experienced, seemed to be the product of a crazed brain.

Even so, she hadn't decided to visit a specialist. She clung to the hope that everything would suddenly revert to normal.

When she realised that Paul had other urgent things to do apart from taking her out for a meal or sitting by her side listening to music, she made up her mind to go back to her own flat. She didn't want the predicament she found herself in to affect her relationship with the man she loved. They'd have time enough to think about living together or – if things went well – to set up home in an even more serious way.

Mary welcomed her back with enthusiasm. She was more than happy to have a friend who would listen to her talking, and devote more care than she did to the cleaning and to generally establishing order. When Emma was away, the flat tended to become uncontrollably dirty: unwashed plates and glasses turned up where you least expected them.

Her first night back in her old room was once more filled with anxiety: she woke several times, trembling and covered in sweat. Again she had that sensation of making an effort to see something, but failing. The inside of a house, a painting… and again those letters, this time a little clearer, in black: A. R. K.

The building – she was becoming ever more sure of it – was the museum, though she didn't remember having seen the galleries with the appearance they had in her dream. As for the people, they undoubtedly wore nineteenth-century clothing. But what was worrying about that? The truth was: nothing – or so she tried to convince herself.

There was one more detail to add to the rest. Whenever she visited the museum and sat opposite the paintings, she saw the same man as on the first day. The difference was that now she simply couldn't explain why he came back again and again, exactly as she did.

She began to observe him and noticed that from time to time he was observing her too. But they always kept their distance.

Emma was already ashamed of what people might think of her. A young woman who spent hours in front of the paintings, her gaze fixed yet absent, as if waiting for a response which never came. Did she look like a lunatic? But what else could she do? She had tried to stay at home working or reading, but couldn't. The anxiety and nervous tension had been so unbearable that she had had to get out of the house, almost at a run. Normally she took great care over her appearance, selecting meticulously from a wardrobe of clothes that were always clean and neatly ironed. Now, though, she was sometimes so impatient to leave that she spent virtually no time getting ready, grabbing the same trousers and pullover she'd left on a chair after wearing them the day before.

That morning was one of those cold and damp October days when the wind in Cambridge strikes you in the face round every corner, as if it had been lying in ambush. Emma headed for the museum as soon as it opened. Two of the custodians greeted her. If they were surprised to see her returning so incessantly, they didn't show it.

She climbed to the first floor by one of the great marble staircases that flanked the desk near the entrance, and for a moment tried to visualise the scene at the museum's inauguration in 1845. There would have been constant activity: visitors viewing the exhibition, dressed for the occasion in all their finery; upper-middle-class men, women and children, mingling with aristocrats and members of the university, writers, professors and artists. The official opening would have been a great event for the city, giving impetus to its cultural life in those years.

Once again Emma believed that she held before her eyes those visitors belonging to another age, like distant ghosts drifting by. Was she dreaming, or was her imagination so powerful that, through the mere act of thinking, she felt herself to be living in the era in which she was so deeply immersed?

She turned her head: everything returned to the twenty-first century. She was now alone in the exhibition room. Just her and the paintings: nothing else. Her favourite was the *Angeli Laudantes* by Burne-Jones, with their dreamy and mysterious expressions. Burne-Jones had been a magnificent artist, a worthy follower of some of the most characteristic traits of those who styled themselves the Pre-Raphaelites, yet already showing signs of his evolution towards what would be the Symbolist movement.

'Excuse me, miss.'

The voice behind her back left her almost breathless.

Emma wasn't expecting it. There he was. Behind her, trying politely to attract her attention. The man who came to the museum every day. Seen from close up, he was more attractive. There was nothing special or threatening about him. An ordinary man.

'Forgive my boldness in approaching you,' he continued, 'but I've been watching you and asking myself why you spend so many hours here. I know you may think I'm interfering, but I'm wondering if you come to the museum to work, or if there's something else…?'

Emma looked at him uncomprehendingly. She knew he had noticed her presence, just as she had noticed his. But she would never have dared to start a conversation.

'I don't want you to think I'm mad,' he went on. His way of speaking and his demeanour were correct, educated. It was clear he didn't mean to harass her. Whatever he had to say to her, it must be important.

'Don't worry,' Emma replied, having recovered from the shock which the man had given her. 'The truth is that I'm writing a thesis on English painting, and there are some works here which interest me particularly – from the nineteenth century, by the Pre-Raphaelites…'

He looked into her eyes as if he didn't believe her and was expecting a more convincing answer. Emma still couldn't make out the point of this conversation. She felt ill at ease and anxious.

'Look, I'm the owner of an art gallery in London. I came to Cambridge for a few days in connection with my work. But I don't know what's happening to me. I've been here for a week, and every day I feel a compulsion to come to this museum, and I can't make up my mind to leave. Something is drawing me here, and I don't know what it is. When I saw you in what I thought was a similar situation, I thought you might be able to help me. I tell you again: I'm not crazy; I live a perfectly respectable life. In fact the people who work for me keep ringing me to find out why I haven't returned yet – I've a load of business waiting for me to attend to.'

Emma couldn't believe what she was hearing. Whatever it was that had taken possession of her, had taken possession of this man too. It seemed to be a contagion. Incredible.

'I don't know what to say,' she replied, 'or how to begin. But you're right. Apart from coming to the museum for my work, in these last days I've experienced exactly what you describe. All day I'm worried and nervous, trying to understand what's happening to me.'

He nodded. Unconsciously, like somnambulists, they walked together and sat down on one of the benches in the middle of the gallery. This unusual situation surely needed talking over more carefully.

How it had all begun, neither of them could say. Gradually more details surfaced of the nightmare they were sharing: the sensation of being in another era, the brutal and overwhelming urge to keep returning to the museum…

Their anxiety seemed to lessen as they unburdened themselves. The tension disappeared, and the tale they were telling became less personal, turning into something which they could now analyse and evaluate.

The dreams. Here too their experiences coincided. Recurrent dreams which, without being overtly threatening or macabre, left a feeling of unease. It might be a memory, buried in their brains. Not a memory of a lived event – they were both too young for that – but maybe a memory of a book read, a film seen…? These were some of the questions they formulated. But their intuition told them that the answer was no. The situation now was even less comprehensible. Before, they might have explained things by a particular emotional state, an illness even. But what kind of illness or emotional state could have identically affected two people who didn't know each other and had nothing in common? What was the point at which they intersected? There must surely be one.

Emma scrutinised the man sitting next to her, and again sensed that there was something familiar about him. In any case, for whatever reason, his presence had reassured her. She felt almost elated, as if she had just met an old friend and had spent the morning in relaxed conversation with him.

He took a business card from his wallet and gave it to her. His formal tone had given way to something more free and easy.

'My name's Julian White. I suppose we'll be seeing each other again if all this carries on. Here's my phone number just in case…'

Emma understood what that "just in case" meant: 'Just in case you discover anything related to what's happening to us.' But what was there to discover? Emma clung to the hope that all this would go away, just as it had come.

'And mine's Emma Carter. I guess you can call me too when you want,' she added, handing him a scrap of paper on which she'd written the number of her mobile.

4

THE VOICES AND THE LAUGHTER, THE MUSIC, THE smell of old wood and beer, all this began to make her forget recent events, transporting her to a different and more real world, which suited a young woman of twenty-four who had gone to a pub with a group of girlfriends.

Mary had gone on insisting until finally she had managed to convince her, after several days during which Emma had stayed in her room like a recluse, rejecting any suggestion to go out and enjoy herself.

Now the two of them were with some other girls, drinking pints and talking about nothing in particular. It had been dark for hours; the warmth inside the pub was comforting. Even so, a few young people were defying the damp and the cold, sitting on benches on a small patch of grass next to the river to have a smoke.

Emma was glad to be there, recovering what seemed far away – a normal life: her nearly completed thesis which would lead to a job; her boyfriend; her moments of relaxation. This time Paul hadn't accompanied her. Tonight it was women only. A night to drink, laugh, gossip and in general to complain about men. For Mary the psychologist, men were full of inconsistencies, secret corners, egoism and fears, naughty children who deserved a special study of their behaviour with the opposite sex. But that didn't mean they weren't also adorable.

Emma laughed. She couldn't complain. She had Paul, with whom everything seemed to be going well. They felt at ease with each other, and shared many tastes and interests. A life with him looked simple and straightforward, without major arguments or problems. Yet she still wasn't sure she wanted that kind of life – or that she wanted it *now.* It was hard for her to commit herself to him completely. It was as if she wanted to leave a door open; but towards what, she didn't know. I'm still young, she told herself.

'At least you've got a guy who loves you and is always superattentive,' said Mary. There was a touch of envy, but without malice.

'Would you like to know what he's like in bed?' Emma winked conspiratorially.

'No thank you, you wicked girl. I don't need to feel worse than I already do about my extinct sex life.'

Emma knew that the whole conversation was designed to make her laugh and put her in good spirits. She was grateful for it. Mary had the delicacy not to press her on what the matter was. If her friend was keeping quiet, well, she would have her reasons – was Mary's attitude.

Yet perhaps Mary was just the person to search for an explanation for these strange events. Emma's talk with Julian that morning had been astonishing, unbelievable. A man who seemed to be completely normal, and who suddenly found himself assaulted by the same visions and sensations as she was. What was there in the museum? What strange force, which you could call supernatural, was arousing within the two of them that restlessness and anxiety to understand or see something they were incapable of understanding or seeing?

That same night, back at the flat, Emma tried to explain the situation to Mary, as they sat on the old sofa with a blanket over their knees. Maybe the pints of beer had helped, and the words poured out more easily, without barriers or embarrassment.

'If I didn't know you, I'd have thought you were completely drunk, or you've gone crazy, or you're having me on,' was her friend's immediate response.

'I know. I'd think exactly the same if someone told me what I'm telling you. But I assure you that what I'm saying about this man Julian is true. My dreams… well, perhaps they're only dreams, perhaps, like you say, it's all because I'm working too hard, spending all day reading about the lives of those nineteenth-century artists. And yet…'

'It might be a clinical illness,' Mary continued, 'and in that case a brain scan would give an answer. Even though what you say is true – that it's very strange that this other person shows exactly the same symptoms at exactly the same time, as if you'd both contracted the same illness at the same moment – still, it might be useful to rule it out,' she added, thinking of recent studies she'd read on the influence of the brain in certain cases of hallucinations. 'I mean, rule out a cerebral pathology.'

Emma looked at her, on the point of bursting into tears. No, she didn't want to be ill. Not now. She couldn't allow it. She was sure there had to be another explanation, however astonishing, however "inexplicable".

'I'll have another talk to Julian,' she said. 'Maybe we can throw some new light.'

Mary felt uncomfortable, sad about the pain she could imagine her friend suffering. Surely she should be able to help her. They'd known each other since they'd first come up to Cambridge and arrived together at Newnham College. They'd shared a lot of experiences.

They went off to bed in silence. They'd probably have a bit of a hangover the next day. A brief "good night" to Justin, who was making himself a cup of tea in the kitchen, and both of them took refuge in the tranquillity of their own rooms.

Emma lay on the bed in the dark, hardly daring to go to sleep. In her mind she rehearsed the things that had happened, analysing them impartially to give herself the chance to find some clues, a place to begin. Her brain was functioning well, she told herself. And her thoughts struggled against the idea of an illness.

A painting. That was the focus of her dreams and her visits to the museum. But what did she see in the painting? She wasn't sure. Indistinct figures, a landscape with trees and water – rather than seeing this, she *felt* it.

What she certainly remembered were those letters, which had been growing larger, black and shining: A. R. K. Might they be the painter's signature? If so, perhaps here was a clue, a beginning along the way to clarification – supposing it truly was a real painting, and a real painter.

A. R. K. She got up from the bed and wrote it on a bit of paper, making up her mind to check it in the library. The idea of embarking on a piece of research revived her spirits.

When she lay down again, the prospect of going to sleep no longer worried her.

Again the same dream, recurring at intervals, mixed up with other sensations and images. This time the outlines were sharper, people dressed in the clothes of another era. Horses, carriages, smoke. A building with tall white columns. A wall filled to the ceiling with paintings, some larger, some smaller.

Emma woke up, drenched in sweat. But she wasn't frightened or anxious, just impatient to start the investigation, convinced now that she had dreamed of something real, something she could trace and discover, just as when she was working on her thesis.

She would go to the museum; that she knew. And she would see Julian. But above all else, and at all costs, she must go to the library.

5

It had been a huge effort, but there was no alternative. It was Sunday, and it was several weeks since she'd promised to go to London to have lunch with her mother. Real life was asserting its claim on her.

It would be a break from the events she found herself immersed in: the museum, Julian, the paintings. She'd left Mary surprised, and Paul worried about her health. They'd both agreed she wasn't well enough to undertake the journey by train and tube to the area in West London where Mrs Carter lived. Suppose she felt dizzy. Suppose she lost consciousness. They seemed convinced that what was happening had something to do with a physical problem, probably her brain.

But Emma hadn't wanted to cancel the lunch. Her mother would be upset, or even frightened if she thought Emma was ill. Emma didn't want to make anyone else anxious about her.

It was true she'd arrived at Cambridge station in a state of nervousness, almost on the brink of a panic attack, when she saw the platform full of passengers waiting for the next train to King's Cross. Young men pushing bicycles, families with children heading for a day out in the capital, tourists visiting England…

A coffee and a muffin from a station kiosk made her feel a bit better. Cradled by the movement of the train carriage, she tried to keep her mind blank, without thinking of the museum, without thinking of anything, focusing on being a student going to spend Sunday with her mother. She searched inside herself for a forgotten memory of happy days spent in London, and she clung to it as a drowning person clings to a lifebelt.

You couldn't say her relationship with her mother was bad; perhaps a bit cold and distant, especially since Emma had become conscious that they didn't have much in common and had been slowly growing further apart. Even so, they kept up the habit of visiting each other now and then, trying to maintain the image of a family which didn't correspond to reality. What is more, Anna Carter wasn't Emma's real mother; Emma had known it since she was fourteen. But that had nothing to do with Emma's feelings for her.

Emma had been adopted soon after birth; she had never known her true parents. The Carters had given her a happy home, and for many years she had no idea that they weren't her real family. She had an elder brother, a natural son of the Carters who now lived in Australia with his wife; he never forgot to send Emma a present and a card on her birthday. Eight years ago her adoptive father had died in an accident. After that, her mother changed completely. In her depression she tried to pour all her frustration and pain onto Emma, provoking in her daughter a feeling of resentment which grew sharper with the years. When Emma left home to study in Cambridge, her mother didn't share her happiness in her academic success; instead she withdrew into herself, and spent a week without leaving the house. At any hour of the day or night Emma would get phone calls from a tearful mother who couldn't bear to see the nest empty.

This was when Emma began to think of searching for her true parents: to find her roots, her family. And now, in that overcrowded train bound for London, she remembered the times she had gone to an agency, ready to pay whatever it might cost to discover her biological parents. So far, without success. But now, more than ever, it might be vital to investigate her origins, to know if all this might be due to a hereditary medical condition.

Her mother greeted her with a smile, almost timidly, as if in all these years she hadn't yet learned how to deal with this daughter who had become so difficult and unfamiliar. It was easy to see there was no genetic link between them: if Emma was thin and diminutive, with straight blonde hair, Anna Carter was a tall and ample redhead, with permanently rosy cheeks and a mischievous smile like a pixie's.

The house was just one more in a row of identically styled properties in a quiet London street. It had obviously been painstakingly looked after. What a contrast to the homely disorder which Emma was used to in her small shared flat. The house smelled of Sunday roast and furniture polish. Everything as usual. Anna hadn't changed at all.

The conversation began with the usual comments on the weather – in England there was always something to say about *that* – and rising prices ("the economic crisis"). They were like two neighbours who didn't share many confidences and had to resort to commonplaces to break an awkward silence.

'And your work? How's it going?' Anna tried to get closer to something like a talk between mother and daughter. 'You look tired. I'm sure your thesis will be brilliant.'

'I've still got a lot to do.' Emma had no intention of opening up and telling her mother what was really happening. But she made an effort to soften her manner, conscious that her mother was only trying to put her at her ease.

The food was delicious: Anna had lost none of her gifts as a cook. As she heard her mother going on endlessly about local affairs, meetings of women's groups in the parish, and her friends, Emma found her thoughts flying to the books waiting for her in her room at Cambridge, books she had borrowed from the library and which she hoped contained a clue to the painting and the initials which she saw in her dreams. She was desperate to read them, to throw herself wholly into research.

'Mum,' she suddenly said, when they had finished eating and she was helping to put the pots into the dishwasher, 'you never told me whether you'd managed to find out my real parents.'

Anna's smile vanished instantly, and an expression of surprise mixed with wariness met Emma's look of expectation. Why bring this up now? They'd discussed this long ago. Surely they'd settled it?

'I never knew who they were, love. We adopted you through an agency – I think your father and I told you so – and the truth is we never bothered about pursuing the matter. You were a healthy baby, your mother couldn't look after you, you know… It must have been one of those young girls who get pregnant. It was the best for everybody.'

Emma lowered her head sadly. She didn't want to be ungrateful, or to hurt the woman who had been her mother for twenty-three years of her life. But Anna obviously hadn't taken much interest in where her adopted daughter had come from, and had assumed circumstances which might or might not have been true. Emma resolved to make some new enquiries. Whether they would get her anywhere, she had no idea. But it was worth a try.

The conversation reverted to banalities, which Emma attempted to follow while her thoughts were already far away. Suddenly she felt an urgent need to go back to Cambridge.

As usual their goodbyes were polite but cold. Anna didn't expect more. Seeing her daughter gave her a strange sensation, a mixture of joy and unease, of comfort and longing.

*

When Emma got back to Cambridge station, it had begun to rain. The sun was going down. She knew the museum would already be shut when she arrived, a thought which left her on the brink of tears.

What she absolutely hadn't bargained for was to see Paul waiting for her. Mary was with him. As ever, she was dressed to attract attention, in a green raincoat and a peculiar brown hat. Emma was touched that they seemed so relieved to see her.

Paul's embrace was warm. He noticed she was tense. Still, she managed to produce a broad smile to dissipate all the fears and bad omens.

'So can someone explain the point of this reception committee?' she joked. 'It's as if I was some kind of celebrity! Where are the reporters and the cameras? I'm not sure I'm ready for a photo shoot!'

Mary took her by the arm and smiled too, even though it was her "serious" smile. She was just glad to see that her friend was OK.

Paul insisted she should spend the night at his house, but she turned the suggestion down. She knew that Paul's love and affection would comfort her, and that he would do everything possible to make her feel well, but she also needed the solitude of her own room, and time to read those library books which might hold the answers to her questions. She certainly didn't want to offend Paul or Mary, but she must get them to realise that she had to confront this alone. Alone? No; with Julian. Julian was the only one who might have access to that extraordinary world which she found herself inhabiting now.

The three of them walked together from the station to the city centre, where Mary and Emma lived. In front of the door of the old building, they said goodnight. Paul was quiet; perhaps a bit disappointed, but he didn't say so. They agreed to talk on the phone the next day.

With Mary too she stayed silent. She went to the kitchen to make herself a cup of tea without saying a word. The trip to London had left her exhausted. Mary sat next to her and looked at her with an expression of discomfort and insecurity, as if Emma had suddenly turned into a stranger with whom she didn't know how to begin a conversation.

Mary watched her lift the cup to her lips and then put it down on the table. Her movements were obviously mechanical. The real Emma Carter was somewhere else.

'Emma,' she said at last.

Emma remained silent.

Mary put her hand on her friend's shoulder. 'Emma,' she repeated, 'are you OK?'

Emma nodded, but the truth was that she had no idea how she felt.

'I've made an appointment for you at the hospital. A friend of mine in Neurology could find the time to do some tests. Maybe the day after tomorrow in the afternoon, if you agree.' And Mary added quickly before Emma could reply, 'Please don't say no; I believe it's something you need to do.'

Although she appreciated Mary's concern, Emma avoided her gaze, head bowed, absent.

'Maybe,' she answered. 'Let me tell you definitely tomorrow. For the moment I've got things to do.'

Mary didn't insist, but told herself she wouldn't leave Emma like this, but would struggle with her to overcome what was tormenting her. Those medical tests would at least be a start.

6

EVEN AT A DISTANCE, SHE RECOGNISED HIM. THE museum wasn't even open yet – another fifteen minutes to go – but Julian was already there on the pavement outside. He looked nervous, taking a few steps, then turning round and walking in the opposite direction, as if he had suddenly changed his mind and remembered he should be going somewhere else.

Emma hurried to meet him. She was sure that he too couldn't wait a moment longer to get to his rendezvous. But who or what was his rendezvous with? With her? With a painting?

They gazed at each other without speaking, each searching for responses from the other.

Then they walked together up the steps to the entrance door, waiting for it to open. At that time in the morning, they were the only visitors.

'You didn't come yesterday,' Julian began.

'No, I went to London to spend the day with my mother. I got back late.'

Emma knew what he was thinking. A day in London? So everything had returned to normal. No more dreams, no more visions.

'Things are just the same,' she went on, guessing the questions he wanted to ask. 'It wasn't a very enjoyable day. But I spent the night consulting some books. I hardly slept—'

He interrupted her. 'Listen, I had exactly the same dream you described. That painting. I can't remember the subject, but I do remember those letters, A. R. K., and today when I woke up – or anyway, I thought I'd woken up – everything was different. Again I saw those people from another time in history. Afterwards I couldn't tell whether it had been a dream or not. It's all so confusing…'

They went into the museum and sat on the bench in the middle of the gallery. The paintings were all in due order, with good lighting for better appreciation. Here was Millais's girl with the wavy hair, over there Burne-Jones's angels. Emma recalled that in the nineteenth century the walls used to be filled with paintings displayed without strict order right up to the ceiling, large oils mixed up with small drawings. The same applied at the Royal Academy in London, where the leading artists of the age had their works premiered and exposed to public scrutiny. The best paintings were hung at eye level, the more readily to be admired.

Emma looked at Julian, and now discovered a little more about the man she had got to know so unexpectedly. She noticed his fair hair and clear, attractive face, with its strikingly shining eyes. Even though his features were tense from the anxiety and embarrassment which this inexplicable situation was surely producing, Emma was convinced that he was an honourable man, one she could trust. For a moment a very female question occurred to her: was he married? But she disguised the smile which came to her lips; after all, this wasn't a date, and the only reason they were together was the strange experience they were sharing. And anyway, there was Paul – her Paul.

As for Julian, he observed the woman sitting next to him as if it was the first time he had seen her. He noticed her high, distinctive cheekbones, the rosy skin of her cheeks, her slender neck. The hands she fidgeted with nervously were small and delicate. And then there was her silky hair, which fell down over her shoulders, and which she drew away from her face with a gesture both automatic and coquettish. In different circumstances he would have watched her laughing carelessly; they would have talked about art, perhaps gone to have tea somewhere. And yet… suddenly Julian felt himself invaded by a strange emotion.

Emma began to talk about her close reading, page after page, of the books she had borrowed from the library in the hope of finding something relevant to her visions. As she spoke, her gaze was fixed on Burne-Jones's angels, as if in their enigmatic expressions she could find confirmation of her words.

Julian listened patiently.

'Does that mean,' he asked at last, 'that you think we're dreaming about something which really happened?'

'Yes. It could be one of these very paintings, but I don't know which one. But I've looked at them carefully and the artists' initials don't match. I tried to find a painter with the initials A. R. K.'

'And?'

'Nothing so far. But that doesn't mean he didn't exist. What I can't explain to you is how this relates to the condition we're in – though I've got the impression it might be a starting point.'

He looked at her again. She seemed so convinced, trying to cling to something solid and real, something that could be explained by a book, just as she would probably do while working on her thesis. Obviously she was a clever and resilient woman, with ideas that were clear and firm. But he didn't yet know what to think. He was ashamed to show himself so vulnerable, so desperate.

'Do you really think this is going to help you solve it?' he asked, perhaps with a tone of reproach in his voice. 'I'm going mad, I can't go back to work, I can hardly sleep… Do you believe you can sort it out just by reading a book on art?'

Emma got up abruptly, as if his words had annoyed her. At that moment her sight seemed to cloud over, as if the visions were returning. Julian had got up too, and instinctively she grabbed his arm. Her unconscious gesture brought her back to the real world.

Julian helped her to walk, his arm round her waist. She felt ashamed. This situation wasn't her fault. They were both suffering equally from the tension of having their lives interrupted, without knowing for how long.

Together they went up to each of the paintings in the room and examined them carefully. They were no longer alone. Some students, notebooks in hand, were walking around the gallery with the restlessness of adolescence.

'I'm going home,' Emma suddenly said, 'to continue the search there. Do you think you'll be OK?'

Julian hesitated. 'Do you fancy getting a bite to eat together?' he asked with a smile. 'I know this is all very disagreeable, but I assure you I used to be a really delightful person.'

Emma smiled too. She had no doubt about what he said, but it would be a strange meal, full of questions. A few months before, she would have enormously enjoyed the company of this mature and interesting man. They would surely have had a lot to talk about. But now…

Yet Emma couldn't resist his anxious expression.

'All right, let's eat somewhere. But let me make some phone calls first.'

Julian couldn't hide his relief. This woman was now the only person who could understand him. He felt incapable of relating to others. He even found it difficult to call London and talk with his colleagues, with gallery owners or with clients. His secretary probably thought he was involved in a sordid affair. And there in Cambridge he felt like an outsider, suspended between two worlds without knowing which way to turn.

Emma reactivated her mobile, which had been on silent all morning. She had three missed calls, two of them from Paul. Obviously he'd been worried that she hadn't rung him.

She tried to return his call, but he had his phone switched off. She tried one more time and finally left a short message on his voicemail: 'Sorry, I'll call you later.' What else could she do?

She went back to Julian and they set off walking side by side. The wind had carried the clouds away eastwards, and a bright sun was warming the street outside the museum.

'If you don't mind a bit of exercise, there's a good pizzeria next to the river,' said Emma, trying to sound cheerful. 'How does that seem? I guess I know Cambridge better than you do.'

'Sure. Take me to a place you like.'

'I'm not sure why, but I'm presuming you'll be used to expensive places. This is a small city, but I like it.'

'You presume wrong. I'm neither an intolerable snob nor a millionaire, if that's what you mean. My business is going well, but it's a business like any other, caught up in the ups and downs of the crisis. Plenty of artists wanting to make money, but not many buyers.'

'I didn't mean to be rude,' Emma hastened to say, 'I was only joking.'

He realised she was trying to turn their stroll together into something agreeable and trivial. On both sides of the street the trees were tinged with yellow and brown, and fallen chestnuts lay open on the grass. Everything invited them to enjoy a beautiful and unusually warm autumn day.

They agreed that a glass of wine would go down well. And so, over a huge pizza and a salad, they started to chat, avoiding any topic which might recall the difficult moments in the museum. They talked of their favourite places in London. Emma spoke about her undergraduate years in Cambridge. Julian, on his side, had studied at a university in the north of England, and had often visited Amsterdam, a city which, as he explained with enthusiasm, he really adored.

Suddenly, in the middle of the conversation, Emma turned her head towards the window. For an instant she seemed to hear a horse's hooves. But there were no horses outside, just two girls on bicycles. When she looked at Julian again, she could tell from his expression that he had heard the same sound.

Once again, events from the past were getting mixed up with the present. Were these strange apparitions, or just the imaginings of their distorted brains?

Yet very soon they were acting as if nothing had happened. They ate with appetite and enjoyed a delicious Italian coffee. Their mood was becoming less tense, more informal. Emma noticed his green shirt and brown jacket; he clearly had a natural taste for good clothes. She also noticed his smooth, fair hair, a bit long at the sides, and flecked with grey. She was sorry not to have taken a bit more care with her own appearance. Julian seemed at ease with her, as he probably was with the people he was used to dealing with. He was a cultivated and pleasant man; the conversation flowed smoothly.

When the meal was over and it was time to go back, Emma found the prospect of saying goodbye difficult. She would have liked to stop time and to stay with him.

The idea of going home was unbearable. Watching the hours pass without knowing what to do…

But there *was* something to do. The books. In spite of Julian's doubts, she wanted to keep on trying.

'I suppose I should be going home,' he said. 'I don't want to waste your time. Until… tomorrow?'

Emma understood his implication. If nothing changed, they would keep meeting in the museum day after day. She didn't know if the thought made her happy or uncomfortable. Each of them was condemned to accept the presence of the other, and to explain to themselves what was happening without knowing if all this was leading them anywhere.

Emma walked in the direction of the building where she lived. The clouds had returned, and the sky was a mixture of greys. Soon it would be raining again.

*

At home, Mary was waiting for her impatiently, almost annoyed.

'I thought something had happened to you,' she said as she opened the door, scarcely leaving her friend time to hang up her jacket. 'Paul has been phoning constantly.'

Emma looked at Mary in surprise, and felt guilty, like a child caught doing something naughty. But she immediately reacted. Wasn't she old enough to do as she wanted? Did she have to account to anyone else for her movements and actions?

'I wish you wouldn't all worry so much about me,' was her response. 'I can't bear it that, on top of all this, you're suffocating me. I have to go on with my life and my work.'

'Your *work*? I get the impression you aren't exactly concentrating on *that*.' Mary was gradually raising her voice. Her words came quickly, jumping from one subject to another. 'And what about Paul? You know he loves you and that he's worried about you. Please, Emma, just try to understand it. Something's happening to you, something we can't ignore.'

Emma flopped down on the sofa. Why couldn't they leave her in peace? The frustration which overwhelmed her, the sense of not knowing what was happening to her, all this wasn't going to get better with so many questions.

At least Julian didn't have friends who were putting pressure on him, she thought. But then she regretted her attitude. She was being very unfair to Mary, and even more to her boyfriend, her partner.

She looked at Mary with tearful eyes. 'Tomorrow I'll go to that appointment at the hospital,' she said. 'I promise.'

Mary smiled, and sat down and put her arms round her. Emma felt comforted by her warmth. Her hair had a familiar scent of jasmine. She must be using the same shampoo as when they were teenagers.

Alice had heard them talking from her room, and came in to say hi. But she didn't ask any questions. She didn't share their intimacy.

'Tea for everybody?' Mary suggested. She sprang up as if trying to block out the impression of what she had said before. She wasn't much of a psychologist if she was pressurising her friend, she thought to herself, a little guiltily. Yet at the same time she believed Emma needed to confront her problem.

Emma said nothing about her meal with Julian. While Mary was making tea in the kitchen, Emma took the opportunity to send Paul a message. Maybe they could meet later?

7

Artists of Victorian England. Nineteenth-Century Painting: Schools and Artists. The Pre-Raphaelites... It was already past midnight. The books were piled on the desk in her room.

Emma had started reading that evening, after a brief, passionate meeting with Paul. As she read, she couldn't stop thinking about Julian.

Would he be on his own? Would he be as desperate as she was?

She missed his company. And this worried her, because in the end it was Julian who brought to her mind the problem which consumed her. In him she saw a reflection of her own anxiety.

She and Paul had talked. She wasn't sure if he was annoyed because of her absences, but she didn't want to tell him about what had happened in the museum, or about the meal by the river. His kisses and caresses had brought her back to a world of normality in which she was simply a young woman enjoying her partner's company.

Afterwards they had gone their separate ways without much explanation, and Emma had returned home ready to continue with her researches. In a moment of lucidity she thought she wasn't sure why Paul put up with it all. She had ignored him, hadn't called him… She wasn't being fair to him. Maybe his love for her was stronger and truer than what she felt for him.

After a few hours of reading her eyes were growing heavy. The lines on the pages were getting confused and turning into a single patch of grey; the paintings in the illustrations were blurred to the point of disappearing.

She tried to focus. No, she couldn't let herself sleep. Sleep would bring more nightmares, more uncertainty.

Dante Gabriel Rossetti made the acquaintance of John Everett Millais through a society called the Cyclographic Club, and in the discussions they had with William Holman Hunt was born the idea of forming their own society, which they called the Pre-Raphaelite Brotherhood. Like every artistic movement, it aroused controversy and scandal…

Suddenly something caught her attention. As she read more details of the lives and works of the Pre-Raphaelites, she came across a brief reference to a painter of the same period who had some connection with them. It seemed he had died quite young, leaving virtually no trace of his work. His name was Knight.

Could he be the artist she was looking for? However, the book told her nothing more. It did, though, include a footnote citing an article by a writer called Caracci: "Rossetti and Other Nineteenth-Century Painters: Their Vision of Women".

Maybe she could find the article in the library. And she could tell Julian... was her last thought before she fell deeply asleep.

*

Next morning she was exhausted. She had slept only a couple of hours, and her sleep had been as disturbed as often before. She couldn't recall what she had dreamed about, but she was sure the painting was still there in her unconscious.

Mary was waiting for her in the kitchen to suggest she went with her to the hospital. Emma hesitated. Was it to make sure she actually went? But she corrected her first impulse of replying abruptly and said nothing, trying to appear amiable to her friend, and also determined and enthusiastic. She wanted to counteract the bad impression which her appearance might give. Depressed and pale, with bags under her eyes, she must be the very image of a sick woman.

Mary prepared coffee, cereals and toast. She too had changed her mood and went back to being her usual cheerful and vibrant self. With her violet sweater and flowered shawl, she brought a note of colour to the kitchen, which was barely illuminated by the first light of day.

An hour later they were in a tiny waiting room, sitting between a man with a violent cough and a young woman with a baby in her arms. Emma couldn't hide her nervousness. It wasn't pleasant to be there, imagining all the suffering around her. Nor did she want to see a doctor, or to have tests, X-rays, give blood, or submit to other uncomfortable possibilities.

Mary interrupted her thoughts. It was another banal conversation, designed to relax the tension. 'Justin is determined to avoid me. I think I'm going to take it as a personal challenge to go out with him.'

Emma followed the thread of Mary's inconsequential chatter. As the minutes passed, other patients came and went through the double doors at either end of the room.

'He's not the Only Man on Earth,' Emma commented, 'and I don't think he suits you. To my taste he's too bound up in his own world. You'd get bored.'

Almost an hour passed before a nurse finally called her name. Mary read the anxiety on her face as she went out.

The tests were endless. Questions and more questions, which she was ashamed to answer. She was afraid they'd conclude she was crazy.

They asked her to undress and put her into an MRI scanner. Meanwhile they were analysing her blood in the lab.

A long while afterwards, a dizzy and confused Emma sat before the desk of the doctor who had examined her. He was an old-ish man, with glasses and a white beard; he sat filling out a form without paying much attention to the young woman in front of him.

'Miss Carter,' he said at last, raising his head. Emma's heart jumped; she was prepared for the worst. 'All the results are completely normal. We'll send you the final results in a few days, but my impression is that you're not suffering from any neurological disease. The blood tests are perfectly in order. Perhaps…' he hesitated, looking at her as if reluctant to go on, 'perhaps you should consider seeing a psychiatrist.'

She couldn't tell whether she felt relieved or distressed. The fact that she was physically well was certainly good news. But it all confirmed that there was something weird and mysterious about her dreams, her visions and her anxiety.

Nor did the prospect of going to a psychiatrist fill her with enthusiasm either. She would talk it over with Mary.

'For now I'm going to prescribe a mild sedative to help you sleep. It will relax you, and maybe you'll feel better.'

Emma smiled, and shook the doctor's hand. 'Thank you, Doctor.'

'Look after yourself.'

Although it was already lunchtime, Emma wasn't hungry. Mary, sitting bored in the waiting room, greeted her joyfully.

There was no need to worry, Emma repeatedly reassured her. But she had decided to use her own methods to investigate the explanation for what was happening to her. There must *be* an explanation.

Mary seemed convinced that the sedative would sort things out.

'Shall we go and eat? I don't start work till three.'

'Let me go to the museum,' Emma implored her. 'I have to talk to somebody.'

Mary's expression made her rapidly change her mind.

'OK. Let's get a sandwich in town. After all those tubes and needles, I guess some food in my stomach will do me good.'

Mary smiled. She was glad to know that her friend wasn't suffering from a serious illness – at least a physical illness. But Mary was also determined to probe the depths of Emma's mind to discover the cause of what was tormenting her. She had known her for years and had found her to be a serious and honest person that you could rely on. She had never shown signs of being unstable, quite the reverse; she was balanced and normal, with the doubts and weaknesses of any human being.

The shopping centre was busy, especially with women of all ages sitting in the cafés or looking in shop windows.

They chose a small eatery on the ground floor of the centre, sat at a table near the door which opened onto the street, and ordered sandwiches and soft drinks. Mary had brought some papers with her; she had to look through them before going to the department where she worked as a part-time assistant while finishing her doctorate. As if that wasn't enough, at weekends she worked with an association which helped unmarried mothers without much money. For Mary, a moment of relaxation was always welcome.

Emma was longing to go to the museum, and also to look out the article which contained details about the painter Knight. She found it strange she hadn't come across his name before.

They ate in silence, ostensibly more relaxed after the experience of the hospital; but each guessed the thoughts of the other.

Finally Mary returned to the theme which had brought them there. 'I'd really like you to talk to me,' she said. 'As your friend. Or as psychologist and patient, if you prefer.' When she saw the hesitation in Emma's eyes, she added, 'You can take your time, you know, till you're ready.'

Emma didn't reply but gave her a broad smile.

A bit later they separated. Mary hurried off in the direction of her College, while Emma made straight for the museum.

'Excuse me, miss.'

'Yes?'

As usual, Emma had arrived at the Fitzwilliam mechanically, only partly aware of her actions. The words of the woman sitting behind the desk at the entrance woke her from a sort of trance.

'I notice that you come here every day,' she said. She was obviously uncomfortable mentioning it but felt obliged to do so. It was her job. 'I wonder if you need any information. We have a Learning Department here for students. Maybe you could contact them…'

Emma followed her drift. The woman was trying to be helpful and was expecting an explanation. 'Thanks very much. I'm writing a thesis, you see, and yes, I do need some information.'

She took the leaflets which the woman handed to her and hurried up the staircase.

Julian had his back to her; he was looking attentively at one of the canvases.

When he noticed her, he couldn't contain an expression of happiness. As if he had been waiting for her.

'You look tired,' he began.

Once again they were the only two visitors in the gallery.

'It all went well at the hospital,' she replied. 'They said I'm fine.'

Briefly she told him about her appointment with the neurologist and the tests they did. She couldn't help smiling at the concerned look in his eyes.

'This morning,' he told her, 'I had the visions again. And I felt the same urge to come here. There was something that was waiting for me – waiting for me to discover it. But what it was, I don't know. I've looked at the paintings one by one, but they don't seem to tell me anything.'

'There's something important I need to show you. Come with me to the library.'

'The library?'

'Yes, my College library.' She spoke in the tone you would adopt with a small child. 'Come on.'

Julian said nothing and let her take the lead.

On the way, Emma explained what it was about. It was all to do with an article on a painter called Knight, which might relate to their dreams. If the content of those dreams had a basis in fact, everything might be more real than they imagined. Even so, that wouldn't explain why their brains kept obsessively returning to a person and an event in the past which they were quite unconnected with.

In the library catalogue it didn't take them long to locate the journal containing the article they wanted. They also soon found a table at which to read it in silence. It was the season when students invaded the reading room, revising their notes or preparing essays.

Emma was constantly aware of Julian's presence as he sat next to her; his closeness produced an emotion in her which she couldn't put into words. Was it because she was on the point of discovering something important? But it wasn't just that. It was a feeling different from anything she had experienced before.

The article summarised the most representative motifs used by the Pre-Raphaelites, as well as their interest in recreating the classical and medieval past through female characters. And indeed it did mention a painter, not well known, by the name of Alexander Knight, who had begun by following the manner of artists such as Maddox Brown and Rossetti, but then developed his own style. He had died very young. Some of his works had been put to auction, but none was housed in a museum in Great Britain. However, it appeared that a small private museum in the USA held an oil entitled *The Lady Isolde*. The author of the article cited the inventory number of this painting and went on to talk about the relationship between Rossetti and the other Pre-Raphaelites.

Julian seemed less enthusiastic than she was. For him, all this data related to something far away and unknown, of interest only to an expert in the history of art. True, his dreams and hallucinations seemed to recreate an era which corresponded roughly to that of the artists they were reading about, but he didn't dare to make a connection. That would be far too astonishing.

However, he wasn't bold enough to contradict Emma.

The article also contained two footnotes referring to other studies of the same theme, as well as details about the private museum where Knight's painting was kept. But another look at the computerised library catalogue convinced Emma that none of these references could be tracked down in the library.

'I'll talk to my supervisor,' she said. 'Maybe he can order the articles for me. He'll think it's for my work.'

And then Emma became thoughtful. Her work... It had come to a standstill for weeks because of all this. Her supervisor had been away at a conference for a few days, but she knew he had begun teaching his classes again. Sooner or later she would have to account for what she had been doing. And that worried her.

'You must be tired.' Obviously Julian had noticed how self-absorbed she was, and he spoke to her in the kind of whisper we all use in libraries. 'Let me invite you for tea; after that I'll take you home.'

She accepted. It was true she was exhausted. It had been an eventful day, and her brain refused to take in any more reflections or ideas. It could all wait till tomorrow.

Being with Julian gave her more and more comfort. She was aware that, though he wasn't in a good state either, he was making an effort to give her support. Perhaps she ought to be doing the same for him.

The hot tea seemed to restore her energy. They had sat in a corner of the library café, a huge room with big windows where the students met when taking a breather from their work.

To have something to talk about, Emma repeated her account of what had happened in the hospital, the questions they had asked her, the tests…

'And I assure you I don't drink,' said Julian, looking straight into her eyes, 'apart from a glass of wine with a good meal, or a beer now and again. And I don't take drugs. When I need it, coffee and tea keep me awake. As you see, I'm a man with quite moderate tastes…' He added, 'In London I used to run. I haven't had health problems. But I see I'm getting old now.'

Emma noticed the intensity of his gaze and turned away to hide what she was feeling. Was it hot in there, or was the warmth coming from inside her?

'Old?' she managed to say. 'You don't look old to me…', and she quickly changed the subject. 'That's why I'm certain that what's happening to us has nothing to do with our physical condition. It's more that some strange connection makes us see the past as if we were present in it.'

'What do you mean?'

'I just don't know. What I do know is that there are people with a special perception, a sixth sense to see things which others don't. There are mediums…'

‘I always thought all that was a load of gibberish for credulous people.’

‘Me too. But there are proven cases. It’s clear that you and I are sensing something, even if we’re not sure what it is.’

For a moment they were silent, trying to take in a possible new perspective on the mystery they shared. Then the conversation became more personal. It was bound to happen. As it did so, it was as if their exhaustion disappeared. They could have gone on chatting for hours, submerged in their own world.

Emma confessed the problems she had with her mother, and the fact that she was adopted. Julian seemed taken aback, and for a moment his expression showed a sadness which Emma couldn’t interpret. But the expression faded, and she couldn’t now tell whether it had been real or she had imagined it.

‘That’s something else I have to follow up,’ she said. ‘I want to trace my real parents. Maybe that way I can find something out about where I came from, something which might help me understand what’s happening to me. Perhaps,’ she went on, with a deliberately mischievous look on her face, ‘perhaps one of my ancestors was burned at the stake as a witch.’

He laughed. ‘I’m sure that whatever happens nothing will alter the fact that you’re a delightful person with a lovely sense of humour.’

Emma again felt uneasy. Without knowing how, she let herself ask the question which was revolving in her mind. ‘And you? Your family? Are you married…?’

Now it was Julian who smiled. And again he had that expression, melancholic and sad. 'All you women want to know the same thing. No, I'm not married. I was once, long ago; but we divorced. These things happen.'

Was it relief, the sensation which immediately came over her?

She didn't know what to reply. She said nothing, thoughtful, burdened with her own emotions.

'I imagine that a girl like you will have some young man to go out with and have fun, planning the future together…'

'Yes,' Emma admitted, in a low voice, as if something in her throat stopped her speaking normally, 'there's someone I've being going out with for a while now. But the state I'm in seems to be making us more distant.'

That's a lie, she said to herself. It was she who was gradually pushing him away from her. And that wasn't fair. At least she owed him an explanation.

'It's late,' she said abruptly, afraid of where this conversation might lead them. 'I'd like to go home. Thanks very much for your company.'

Julian looked at her again with that sad expression which seemed suddenly to have seized him. He really didn't comprehend what was happening, and while one part of him desired to stay at Emma's side, to protect her and help her, another part of him was desperate to run away, return to London, and get back to his daily routine. This woman was beginning to turn his life upside down, as much as or more than those strange dreams which held him captive in Cambridge. And he wasn't sure if that was what he really wanted.

They left the library together, and Julian kept his promise to take her home.

When they got there, they were once more lost for words. They were starting to get to know each other, to feel at ease in each other's company, yet something disturbed the relationship and prevented them from behaving like two normal people, a man and a woman who, in spite of their difference in age, had discovered that they had a lot in common.

'I'll tell you tomorrow if I've found out anything else,' she said. 'In the books, I mean.'

'OK. See you tomorrow,' he added. 'In the museum, I suppose.'

8

After various phone calls and a long wait, she managed to contact the person she wanted.

A female voice at the other end of the line took her personal details and fixed an appointment for the following week.

That morning Emma had been in the museum but had then hurried off, leaving Julian perplexed and uncertain what to do.

Once back home she had searched online till she found an agency which specialised in locating missing persons and in investigating the whereabouts of children and relatives in connection with inheritance. In Emma's case the aim was to trace her real parents, who for some unknown reason had placed her for adoption somewhere in London.

She couldn't provide them with much information to start the search, but she was confident that it wasn't totally impossible. Her date of birth, her adoptive parents, the local registry office where they processed her papers – all this was at least a beginning.

At noon, after a rushed lunch of pasta salad with spicy sauce, and a coffee which burned her tongue, she took her rucksack with the library books in it and headed for the university. She knew her tutor would be in his office in less than half an hour.

She hadn't wanted to contact him by email, preferring to talk in person. That way she knew she wouldn't have to wait for his response.

Emma loved walking by the huge lawns along the backs of the Colleges. In places the brilliant greens of the grass took on darker hues where the trees gave shade. There were scatterings of leaves, some yellow, some brown; at times, when the wind blew, they began a frenetic dance as if to a music which only they could hear. The lawns hadn't altered much from those through which generations of students had walked in centuries past.

Her tutor, a Professor by the name of David Ford, was soon to retire. He had always inspired enormous confidence in Emma since she went to his lectures on the History of Art in her second undergraduate year – which now seemed long ago. Affable and extraordinarily intelligent, he didn't always get on with his pupils because of his character, which was somewhat abrupt and bad-tempered. But with Emma he had always been on the best of terms. From the outset there had developed between them one of those invisible bonds which link us inexplicably to people when we least expect it. For

Emma it had been a pleasure to work with him and learn from him, and she admired him profoundly. So she felt very uncomfortable now about the idea that she had to deceive him.

Nevertheless, he received her with an amiable smile and a relaxed manner which immediately communicated itself to Emma.

They had a talk, a long talk, like old friends. But Emma was impatient to guide the conversation towards the subject which interested her.

'I read your most recent pages. They're excellent.'

'The truth is,' she admitted, 'I haven't worked much for the last few days. I've not been well.'

'Nothing serious, I hope?'

'No, I'm OK.'

Then she took some pages out of her rucksack and showed them to him. They were the notes she had taken about Knight.

'I'd like to find out more about this painter,' she said. 'And if possible, to get images of the works by him which survive.'

If Professor Ford noticed the excessive anxiety in his pupil's voice, he didn't show it. He took the papers she gave him and read them attentively.

'Fine,' he said at last, 'I'll see what I can do. He doesn't seem to be a very important artist, but it will be interesting to check his contribution in comparison with the other painters of the period.'

When he carried on talking about nineteenth-century art, and some sketches in the Victoria and Albert

Museum, Emma followed his words rather mechanically, without paying much attention. The truth was that, although she always enjoyed her tutor's company, this time she really did want to get away.

She thanked him profusely, pretending to have a non-existent appointment, and went out of his office.

When she got into the street, the sky was already dark. At this time of the year the evening fell rapidly; the low clouds, laden with rain, had hidden the last flicker of daylight which preceded night. As she walked she felt gusts of damp wind in her face, which made her shudder. Still pondering her recent conversation with her tutor, she crossed the street towards the pavement with better lighting.

How dark it was! And how silent.

All of a sudden it seemed as if the whole world had disappeared, and that she was the only living soul, the last survivor in a ghost city.

She quickened her step, anxious to get to the warm and bustling area where she lived, where there was always a café, a shop or a pizzeria open.

But now she didn't recognise her surroundings. Was she lost?

She turned a corner and saw a man and a woman coming towards her. At last, she thought, there was someone else in that deserted street.

But as they came towards her she realised that something wasn't right. Their movements and dress showed her immediately that they weren't what one would expect to see on a late October evening in the early twenty-first century.

This man and woman belonged to a different era.

They passed her by silently, like shadows.

When she turned to look the other way, there were more people, of similar appearance, walking along the opposite pavement.

She couldn't tell whether at that moment she cried out or just opened her mouth breathlessly to try to utter a sound which never reached her lips.

She shut her eyes. When she opened them again, a young man was holding her by the arm.

'I'm sorry, I'm really sorry. I didn't see you. I thought…'

He was wearing jeans and a grey sweatshirt, and had just got off a bicycle. It seemed he had been on the point of running her over.

'Are you OK?'

Two other boys came up. In front of them shone the lights of a café. The traffic signals were at green, letting a line of cars go through. At the corner, behind its glass screen, gleamed the circular, golden shape of the clock which had become one of the prime attractions of Cambridge. A strange clock, presided over by a monstrous insect which its creator had named the "Chronophage" – The Devourer of Time.

'I'm fine,' said Emma, on the verge of tears. 'I'm sorry I was in the middle of the road. I tripped. I wasn't looking where I was going…'

The hallucinations had returned. And this time, how real they had been. She was still trembling with terror.

She was sure she had seen those people, sure she had experienced something strange and uncanny in the street where she was walking, a street totally unlike the way it looked in the present moment.

She turned to gaze at the insect on the clock and smiled at it, glad to see its familiar appearance, which had brought her back to the world of today.

When she got back to her flat – she still wondered how she managed it – she went straight to her room. She lay on her bed and let her eyes fill with tears, which ran freely down her cheeks till she felt them, cold and wet, on her neck. There was no one to hear her sobbing. No one to realise how frightened she was, since at any moment she risked losing her sense of reality without being aware of the fact. In recent hours she had been so optimistic, convinced that painstaking research into some books could lead her to uncover the truth. Now, all that had disappeared at a stroke. The assurance that she didn't have a tumour or a cerebral disease which might be affecting her senses, now seemed unimportant.

Her tears gave way to complete exhaustion. In a few minutes she was deeply asleep.

*

She awoke with a start when her mobile rang, at the same time as Mary opened the door of her room.

Emma didn't react at once. She had no idea how long she had been asleep. When she eventually managed to find her phone so as to reply, it was no longer ringing.

'What's wrong? Are you OK?' Mary sounded anxious, understandably surprised to have found Emma in her room and looking as she did.

Emma switched her gaze from Mary to her mobile and back again, without knowing what to do. She was still drowsy, halfway between the worlds of dreaming and reality.

The screen of her mobile showed the missed call: Paul.

No. Now, she couldn't face a conversation with Paul. It would be equally hard to come up with explanations and to pretend that nothing was wrong.

'Come on, love, what's happened?'

Mary's affectionate hug made her react at last. She got up from the bed and went to sit at the seat by her desk. Mary moved a pile of clothes and went to sit as close as possible to her, on the coloured quilt they had bought together in a charity shop.

'I must look ghastly,' Emma stammered, conscious of her reddened eyes, her cheeks blotchy with mascara, and her hair in a mess. 'I think I need a shower and some time to sort my appearance out.'

'Don't worry about beautifying yourself.' Mary's expression was somewhere between irony and amusement. 'Luckily for you, you were born good-looking, unlike others – including me. But joking aside, it's obvious something serious has happened. Is it to do with Paul?'

'No.' She was silent for a time, while Mary waited patiently. Finally she related what had happened. As she told her story, it seemed to her more and more incredible. Yet it had been so real…

'And the sedative?'

'I haven't taken it yet. I wanted to keep my head clear for some important things.'

'It's obvious that what's happening to you isn't normal. I'm worried. I'm beginning to think you really might possess psychic powers, even if it could all still be due to stress or some sort of trauma.'

As they talked, Emma felt herself relaxing. She knew she could trust Mary, and that her advice would be the best possible. Still, she was struggling to find a way forward on her own, relying on nothing but her own resources.

'Maybe it's the extreme stress of writing the thesis,' Emma commented, with a half-hearted attempt at a smile. 'I know I've been working hard, but it was all going well. I enjoy my work, and I'm trying to get the very best out of the grant they've given me. After all, *you* never stop working either. And look at Justin and your friends…'

'I know,' said Mary. 'It all seems normal. Is there anything else you haven't told me?'

Emma hesitated. 'Actually, yes. And it's precisely got something to do with what's happening, even though it's something I've been thinking about for some time. I want to find my real parents.'

Mary stared at her with astonishment and incredulity. She knew about Emma's family situation. As students they had spent hour after hour chatting. Each knew almost everything about the other's life: boyfriends, parents, friends… They had often laughed as they remembered details about their occasional boyfriends. And Emma knew by heart the adventures of Mary's parents, who in a fit of madness had upped sticks and gone to live on the Mediterranean coast of Spain, where they cultivated their own vegetable patch and led a tranquil life virtually secluded from civilisation. But Mary found it hard to comprehend that at this late stage Emma wanted to uncover something which belonged to a far-off past without apparent relevance to her present life.

'Suppose it turns out that my mother or father had experienced a symptom similar to mine? Mightn't that help to explain what's happening to me? Lots of things are down to genetics…'

'I don't know,' Mary replied. 'But perhaps it's the other way round. Maybe *this* is what's causing your problems. Anxiety and fear of the unknown, of what you might find out. Do you want me to prepare something for you to eat?' she added. 'We can carry on talking in the kitchen.'

Emma agreed with a smile. Mary was obviously peckish, as she almost always was. Her mother would also have thought that a good meal was the answer to all the world's troubles. Her mother… Why had the image of Anna and the dishes she cooked suddenly come into her mind?

They sat at the kitchen table. But before Mary had time to pile generous slices of bacon and chips on their plates, Emma's mobile rang. This time she had no reason to ignore it.

'Emma?'

It was Paul.

'Yes. Hello, Paul. How are you?'

'I get the impression you're ignoring me, and I don't understand why,' was the reply on the other end of the line. 'I'd like us to have a quiet talk, but I see it's getting very difficult. Do you want me to come to see you?'

'No.'

'But what's wrong? Am I to blame for something?' His voice rose a little.

'I'm sorry, I'm really sorry,' was the only thing she could say. She herself couldn't tell why she was doing this to him. But she knew she couldn't take a backward step.

'I'm so sorry you aren't well, but if you don't want anything to do with me, it's better if we're honest about things as soon as possible.'

Emma couldn't disagree. She suddenly felt nothing for the man she thought she had been in love with. Nor did she miss his kisses, or the nights spent in his arms. With her mobile still in her hand, staring at it as if it were an unfamiliar object whose purpose she didn't comprehend, she realised that the kisses she longed for were those of someone else, and that until she received them her heart would not be wholly satisfied.

Mary was looking at her, even more astonished if possible, unable to credit what she was hearing. The bacon was getting cold in the pan.

Paul rang off without saying more. Emma knew it would be very hard to regain the love of the man who had been her boyfriend, her hope for the future.

'But *why*?' Mary asked. 'What has all this got to do with Paul?'

Emma couldn't find a reply. She knew he would be crushed by her rejection, but she had been honest. There was no reason to maintain their relationship as if nothing had happened, with Paul ringing her or trying to see her, while she was inhabiting another world. A world in which the only person who existed was Julian. A world in which past and present intermingled.

'I don't have the strength to keep a relationship going now,' she said at last. 'Maybe it's better this way. To give ourselves some time and see what happens. It wouldn't be fair for me to pretend.'

Mary looked at her again sadly. 'I thought that it would do you good to be with him, that the love and support he could give you would be some help. I'm sorry it's not like that.'

Emma sensed that things were getting more and more complicated. How could she talk to Mary about Julian? What madness was this? Not only were there times when she seemed to be living in the nineteenth century, but she was falling in love with a man who had the same symptoms as she did.

'I'm not hungry,' she said, her stomach turning over at the very thought of the bacon and chips still lying in wait in the pan. 'I think I'll go to bed.'

Mary agreed this was best. Her friend seemed so pale… She had never seen her like this.

Once in her room, Emma picked up the last of the books she had been reading. So many things were turning over in her mind. The anxiety was almost unbearable.

She fell asleep with the book still in her lap. And this time her dream was even more intense, more real.

She saw with absolute clarity a room in a museum, and people dressed in the style of 1800: men in dark suits, with hats and walking sticks; women – surely from the upper class – wearing long, ample and brilliantly coloured dresses, accessories, and adornments. They all seemed very pleased to be there, as if participating in an important event. As they walked from one side to another, Emma imagined rather than heard their laughter and their animated conversation. She wanted to know what they were talking about, to ask them what they were doing there, but she couldn't. Something prevented her.

When she woke up, as usual with a start and with a tightening of the throat, the first impression she had before her dream faded in her memory was – this she was completely sure of – that everything she had seen in her vision she had witnessed from within the interior of a painting.

Ely

November-December 1858

1

ALEXANDER HAD TAKEN HIS TIME SETTLING INTO the old house, which was now gradually coming to life and taking on the look of a home.

The study had become a warm corner where he felt completely at ease, intoxicated with the smell of paint, sometimes working feverishly, sometimes desperate that he couldn't achieve the effect he wanted.

The truth was that he hadn't made much progress with the new painting. Days had passed, and although he had done some pencil sketches to compose the scene, he still wasn't satisfied with the results.

Even so, the painting was there in his mind, and all he had to do was wait for the moment when he could make it real, transmitting to the canvas what were still no more than vague impressions.

At the same time he had been working on some drawings which he had brought from London, especially portraits which he had copied from models in Gabriel's studio and which he could incorporate later into other works.

Gabriel's spirit still hadn't vanished. The time Alexander had spent in London was still present in his life.

But this hadn't prevented him from beginning to have his own experiences in Ely, trying to pick his life up from where he had left it. He had some friends whom he used to meet for lunch at the hotel in the High Street; they talked about events of the day, and he kept up to date with the latest local news.

He had even had the honour of being included in the circle of acquaintances of a lady who had been married to a member of high London society. Longing for the life of the big city which she had had to abandon for economic reasons, this woman tried to cultivate people she could refer to as "interesting". As an artist recently arrived from London, Alexander fitted the bill perfectly.

Although she was over sixty, Lady Hunter had the vitality of a teenager. She was a bundle of contradictions. Her small, wizened face contrasted with her sweet, girlish smile; her body looked fragile, but her hands were strong and her voice deep and melodious. She lived on the outskirts of Ely, in a grand house which she had inherited from her ancestors, where she aspired to live the life of the aristocracy. There she gathered together a mixture of types, including a banker, a couple of businessmen from nearby Cambridge, and a lady with a daughter of marriageable age. This lady claimed descent from the nobility, and, like Lady Hunter, was nostalgic for city life in place of this rural existence.

Alexander had been accepted into the group because, in the words of the hostess herself, he was "indispensable" at their gatherings. What an honour for them to have a famous artist amongst them! Even though he didn't consider himself to be famous, he had accepted the offer, more to have something to do when he wasn't working than out of any real interest in these people, who seemed to him vain, superficial and boring.

That evening in the middle of November, when winter was approaching and nothing was more pleasing than a comfortable armchair next to the hearth, Alexander had dined at Lady Hunter's. Now he was enjoying a glass of sherry, listening to the monotonous conversation of two gentlemen telling each other about their "escapades" as young men. He was in no hurry to go home. The combined warmth of the fire and the drink gave him a particularly agreeable sensation, and although these people's chatter didn't fascinate him he was certainly at his ease, lulled by the murmur of their voices. The women, sitting together at the other end of the room, all seemed to be talking at once.

'And you, Alexander, are you painting anything in particular at the moment?' One of the men, the one sitting on his right, looked at him expectantly. He was small and chubby, nearly bald, but with an elegant grey beard which gave him the appearance of an elderly gnome. Alexander recalled that when they were introduced he described himself as a retired banker and a member of the House of Lords.

'To tell the truth, I am,' Alexander replied. 'I have an oil painting to finish, and I intend to do some more over the coming months.'

'I would love to see your work!' His Lordship responded. 'I am very interested in art. I believe it comforts the spirit.'

Alexander smiled good-humouredly but said nothing, unsure whether the man's interest was genuine or whether this was just a way of bringing him into the conversation. Until now he hadn't felt sufficiently at ease in his new surroundings to talk about himself and his experiences. Timidity combined with lack of practice had made him reluctant to become more intimate with them, even though, in their way, they never ceased to be courteous with him.

'A few years ago,' continued the man with the beard, this time after taking a sip of his drink, 'I had the good fortune to be present at the opening of the museum in Cambridge built in memory of Richard Fitzwilliam. I knew his son, you know. The father was a great collector of art.'

Alexander had heard about him, though he couldn't remember where. His mind drifted to another museum, one he knew well: the South Kensington Museum in London. From there his thoughts wandered again, in a fraction of a second, to the Royal Academy of Art, where William and Gabriel had exhibited their works. At that moment such a world had seemed unattainable, but there were other museums and – why not? – other opportunities. You never knew where fate would lead you.

'It will be a pleasure for me to show you my paintings,' he answered at last, with a mixture of humility and pride, 'and to offer you a cup of tea in my house.'

The bearded gentleman, whose name was Lord Robinson, seemed seriously interested. Alexander no longer hesitated to tell him about the period when he had been painting in London. His interlocutor's interest turned now to real admiration. The discussion of art extended through the whole room, reaching the women too, and producing a sudden silence.

'Painting in London! My dear Knight, you must be a great artist then, one of the very finest! How fascinating!' exclaimed the mistress of the house, with an exaggerated gesture which aimed to show everyone her familiarity with the topic.

'Fascinating!' echoed another.

'Perhaps one day you might paint a portrait of me, and another of my dear Susanna,' added a third woman, heavily set and somewhat younger than Lady Hunter; her name was Katherine Morgan, and she was attempting by any means possible to introduce her daughter into society, in spite of that young woman's indifference to the idea. 'My husband would be delighted. And he would pay you well.'

Alexander did not reply immediately, rather overwhelmed by the sudden enthusiasm which his person had aroused. A portrait? He had never thought of painting portraits to commission – that wasn't his style – but perhaps it was something he could bear in mind. Suddenly these people, who at the outset had seemed rather cold and boring, had taken on a new dimension. Work. Men and women with influence. It was the opportunity he needed now.

The conversation rapidly changed direction, and some of Lady Hunter's guests decided that it was getting late and that they had simply no choice but to leave. But *certainly* they would meet again to dine very soon.

Alexander arrived home soaked and almost frozen. Mrs Smith wished him goodnight and retired discreetly. All was prepared: a nice fire was burning in the hearth and there was hot water in his room. Outside it was still raining.

He changed his clothes, but instead of going to his bedroom he decided to spend a while in his studio. He wasn't tired, or at least not tired enough to go to bed and sleep straightaway. The events of the evening: the dinner, the people he had met at Lady Hunter's house, and in particular the conversation about his work, had filled him with optimism, as if he were on the point of beginning something important. If only one day he could gain the prestige he dreamed of...

He would probably accept the offer to paint Mrs Morgan's portrait. Although this would mean a delay in his work on the Adonis canvas, he was sure it would be worthwhile.

He contemplated the pictures which leaned against the walls, with the tenderness of a father gazing at his children. Here were his sketches, his drawings, his oils, with those contrasts in colour which he had learned from his masters, and which made the images resemble medieval stained glass.

All at once he stopped, when he reached a painting still wrapped in a piece of white fabric. It had remained untouched since he had moved house. His heart leaped.

He well knew what he had painted, but it still took an effort for him to see it again. That was why he had tried to keep it hidden. He hadn't dared to destroy it, but nor did he have the courage to look once more at the face of the woman who had been his model.

Elizabeth...

How much beauty lay in those rosy cheeks, those lips with their promised warmth and moistness, those clear and dreamy eyes!

In truth he had no need to look at the painting to hold her image perfectly clearly in his mind. She was the reason he had broken off what might have been a long career as a painter in London and had returned to his home town. To escape her influence. To avoid being carried away by his feelings and destroying a friendship which he valued more than anything in the world.

From the first moment he saw her he knew how important Elizabeth Siddal was for Gabriel. You only had to look at them to realise the passion which had arisen between these two extraordinary people. A passion whose power you could almost physically sense when you were near them, like an aroma or a breath of warm air, as he painted her and gazed at her with feverish eyes, while she posed voluptuously. It was like being present at an act of love.

Both shared the same inspiration, and sometimes they worked together, as if vying with each other to see which of them could achieve the more sublime creation. Elizabeth had not just been a model. She was also an artist, a painter, a poet. A beauty capable of engendering beauty. But also of engendering the most powerful and destructive emotions in the men who surrounded her.

There they had been: Gabriel, William, Edward and Elizabeth, drawing, painting, writing. And with them, he, Alexander, had learned to portray that perfectly curved female body. But nothing more. As soon as he became aware that his hand trembled and his heart pounded when he was with her, he decided he could no longer continue. Elizabeth belonged to Gabriel. And Gabriel was his friend and his master.

Suddenly he felt a wave of heat rising into his cheeks. Perhaps the fire had been burning in his studio for too long.

Alexander took out the canvas and forced himself to look one last time at the face of Elizabeth, in her portrayal of a woman in medieval costume. One last time. He couldn't go on tormenting himself by imagining what might have happened if he had allowed his feelings free rein.

He grabbed his brushes and painted over the image, coat upon coat, till Elizabeth disappeared completely.

2

My Dear Gabriel,

I do not know if this letter will find you in London, at your usual address, or elsewhere.

How different everything has been since my arrival! How many new things to get used to: the people, the town, so small that after a short walk you have covered all of it. Still, it has its own kind of charm, and I have rediscovered things I had forgotten from years ago. I love visiting the wonderful cathedral, admiring the shape of every last arch and column, the formal perfection of its corridors, the rich hues of the glass (how you would love it!). It is also agreeable to be surrounded again with memories of my family. It gives me the sense of having roots somewhere.

The most important thing now is my work. I have plans to do a painting which I know will be good, a real "son" for you, which I hope will not disappoint those of you who believed in me. I am also working for a delightful family who have commissioned some portraits. At first it seemed very difficult, but I am gradually seeing myself moving in the right direction and feeling very proud.

I don't know if the Oxford paintings have gone ahead. I know the high hopes you had for them. I trust that William, Edward, John and the rest are all well. From my secluded little corner, be assured you have my greetings and my eternal gratitude.

Alexander

The day had dawned cold and unpleasant, with ice on the windows and a pallid, yellowish sky.

He had sat next to the fireplace where Mrs Smith had served an excellent breakfast. As he sat drinking a steaming cup of tea, Alexander had decided to write at last a letter to the friend he pined for, Dante Gabriel Rossetti. For a time he had been hesitating, consumed with the need to contact him, but unwilling to resurrect memories of a past which now seemed far off. But eventually he had taken paper and ink. As he wrote, he felt himself transported to that house, to that room which the two of them had decorated together, a room filled with objects which seemed to have been plucked from another age: painted chests, seats with legs twisted like those in a church, curtains sporting flowers and exotic birds.

Would the letter reach him? Certainly – unless his volatile spirit had led him once more to move house, or his hectic life had dragged him on a journey with no destination in view.

What he dare not confess even to himself was the question which set his heart palpitating. How was Elizabeth? Were they still together?

But now that didn't matter. Even if – as he always suspected, and as friends confirmed – there were other women in Gabriel's life, all that lay in the past.

After finishing breakfast he put the letter in an envelope and left it carefully on the table. As he did so he couldn't help smiling with pleasure as he saw the little painted wooden box placed in the centre. A present from Edward Burne-Jones, a habitual and almost obsessive collector of artistic objects.

Alexander had spent most of the week visiting the house of Lady Hunter's friends the Morgans. The portrait of Mr Morgan was already well advanced, and everyone seemed very satisfied with his work. He had made some sketches from life of all the family, including the daughter Susanna, and he was now spending his evenings painting in oil, observing how these people whom he now knew well were gradually taking shape, coming to life on the canvas in his own house. A commission which at the beginning had seemed monotonous and uncreative had turned out to be full of interest. And Lewis Morgan had proved to be a man full of energy and with a refreshing sense of humour. He was rather handsome and still quite young, and he posed with absolute patience.

There always seemed to be some fresh news. At lunchtime the previous day Mrs Morgan had mentioned enthusiastically that an old friend of hers, who had just moved to England from South Africa, was going to spend a while in Ely with her family.

'Obviously the first thing I did was to talk about *you*, my dear Alexander,' she had said. 'I'm sure she would love to meet you. And perhaps they would want some portraits done…'

Alexander had smiled. He knew that Katherine Morgan had taken him under her wing and had decided to help him obtain a position as a painter. If he had to start by painting all the well-to-do women who lived in the area, what did it matter? Venus and Adonis could wait a little longer.

So he had agreed to accompany the Morgans to take tea that afternoon. He would meet the Stevensons and talk once again about his work and his art. He was beginning to grow accustomed to the interest which his personality aroused in this rural setting which in recent years he had almost forgotten.

On the stroke of three the coachman arrived to collect him for the drive to a country house south of Ely: it was the residence of the Stevensons, now returned to the land of their birth.

By this time the sky was already darkening, and the first tiny stars were peeping out of a cloudless sky. You could sense the frost which would fall during the night.

The journey wasn't a long one, and soon Alexander found himself in the hallway of a large mansion. He was welcomed warmly by the mistress of the house, a tall, well-dressed woman with a natural manner. If at any time he had felt anxious or uncomfortable, Katherine

Morgan (who had already arrived at the Stevensons) soon made it her business to present him to everybody and to put him at his ease.

'Delighted to make your acquaintance, Mr Knight! It's a pleasure to meet you.'

'The pleasure is mine, Mrs Stevenson. Thank you so much for your generous invitation.'

'My husband doesn't enjoy this kind of get-together,' commented the hostess, as soon as the formalities were over. 'But I want to make some friends in the community. When you find yourself somewhere for the first time, you know...' She added, 'Please, call me Margaret.'

'And my name is Alexander.'

He greeted both women with genuine enthusiasm, and was guided to the dining room where four other people were already seated: a tall, fair-haired and extremely thin man, another man who was old and almost bald, and two young women. They interrupted whatever they had been talking about and greeted Alexander effusively.

He sat down at the table. Gradually the awkwardness of the situation – a strange place, unfamiliar people – gave way to an agreeable certainty that he was welcome, that he was among friends.

They offered him delicious sandwiches and pastries which melted in the mouth. A huge chocolate tart dominated the table.

But suddenly everything around him lost importance when he caught sight of the young woman sitting opposite him. She could be no more than eighteen, but she had the manners and bearing of an older woman. When she realised that Alexander had noticed her, she lowered her eyes timidly. As she did so, her hands, which held a cup of tea, trembled slightly. Was it his imagination, or had the girl become nervous?

He looked at her openly and smiled. She smiled too. She let her gaze rest on him for an instant, and then, embarrassed, looked away again.

For a while, detached from the conversation which was going on around them, Alexander and the young girl played a game of glances which gradually became bolder and more direct. It seemed she had regained her composure: her hands were steadier, her eyes more vivacious.

How pretty she was. Alexander delighted in contemplating her silky, lustrous, fair hair; her smooth, slightly rosy cheeks; her little nose; and the smile, somewhere between serious and mischievous, which, now and then, inadvertently, came to her lips.

He knew she was the younger daughter of the owners of the house: Ariadne Stevenson – that was how they had introduced her to him. She clearly came from a good family, had been educated in both England and South Africa, and was used to behaving with discretion and modesty when in the company of men. But what he also saw in her, he couldn't tell why, was a character both strong and tenacious.

He could have gone on watching her for hours, filling himself with the sweetness which emanated from her whole person, a sweetness which not even the most delicious chocolate tart could equal. Yet he had no choice but to pay attention once more to the other people at the table, and to respond to the curiosity which his paintings had again aroused. In the midst of Mrs Morgan's constant eulogies, her friend had already made it clear that she would love Alexander to paint her portrait.

Alexander agreed with pleasure. Suddenly he was becoming a celebrity. And the idea of painting for these distinguished families became more and more attractive.

Painting…

At that moment he imagined Ariadne Stevenson posing for him. But not for the kind of family portrait which her parents would hang over the fireplace. No; it would be for the painting he had been dreaming of for so long. Her face would be the face of the beautiful Myrrha, dominated by an innocent but shameful passion. Or else it would be the face of Venus, whose beauty no mortal woman could surpass.

He was almost dreaming, abstracted in his own thoughts, when he realised that Mr Stevenson was talking to him. He was interested in the social life of London, which for reasons of work he had left behind many years before. Alexander noticed the extraordinary likeness between him and his daughter: the same deep blue eyes, the same expression in his face, the same smooth, fair hair – though in his case it was short and sparse. He recognised those hands too, a masculine version of Ariadne's delicacy and fineness. *His* face, too, would make an appearance in one of the characters imagined by Alexander.

The conversation went on for the rest of the evening. His hosts seemed enchanted to hear the latest social and political gossip from London. They talked about art, and about the great interest which Prince Albert seemed to take in the latest artistic developments. Alexander related what he knew of the Westminster prizes, which years before had been awarded to great painters.

When the evening was over they fixed a date for Alexander to begin work. They would sit for him for some sketches; they could even, if they liked, visit him at his studio. The fee which they offered was larger than Alexander could ever have imagined.

Ariadne said goodbye to him with the same smile – half-timid, half-provocative – that she had fleetingly given him when their eyes met at the tea table. And now Alexander noticed that her delicate white cheeks were tinged with red. Her hands were trembling again.

'Ariadne,' he dared to say, 'you have a very special beauty. It will give me the greatest pleasure to paint you.'

She raised her eyes.

'Thank you. And for me it has been an honour to meet a great artist.'

3

TWO WEEKS HAD PASSED. WINTER WAS APPROACHING ever closer. The days were shorter, the wind more bitter.

Alexander had been painting portraits. Two he had already finished, and he was already planning the composition of a third: the posture of the neck, the mouth, the eyes… As he worked, he was developing new techniques, and at the same time strengthening his friendship with the two families. With Lewis Morgan he had found that he had much in common, and he really enjoyed his company. James Stevenson was more reserved and colder, but always amiable and attentive. What was more, he had a very interesting face which made him easy, indeed inspiring, to paint. Though perhaps what truly made him inspiring was the essence of his daughter Ariadne which Alexander saw in him.

She also had come to his studio a few times. And although her mother always accompanied her – it wasn't proper for a young girl to visit a gentleman's house alone – Ariadne would manage to escape. At the same time her mother didn't seem to mind too much, as if in truth she was trying to encourage their meetings.

One day, while he was painting, Ariadne had sat by his side, so close that he could sense the fragrance of her perfume, a subtle aroma of roses.

What a suggestive face she had. Alexander was captivated as he looked at her, with the aim of trying to reproduce her features on canvas. She laughed. The bashfulness of the first moments had disappeared.

'I like seeing you work, Alexander.' Ariadne was completely relaxed in her conversations with him, something which surprised and moved him. 'I think your paintings are magnificent.'

'And you are a wonderful model,' he replied with a smile. 'But please, keep still for a moment. Don't change your expression.'

He could barely concentrate. Ariadne could be so unsettling.

'Where did you learn to paint like this?'

'I have always longed to paint. For many years. It was my great ambition. My father would have preferred me to choose another profession, but I already knew what I wanted.'

'And you were in London.'

'Yes, I was in London. I studied with great artists who taught me to paint from life, like this. One day I'll show you some of the drawings which they did for me.'

Alexander felt completely happy in the company of this young woman. The two of them were alone in the studio. The painting was gradually taking shape, with each brushstroke.

'Come,' he said suddenly. He took her hand and helped her down from the stool she had been posing on.

'What is it? What do you want?' Ariadne burst out laughing while he walked around her, carried away by an impulse that was almost childlike. He spun her as if in a dance, then laid her down on the rug in the centre of the room. Then he rushed towards her carrying a pile of coloured fabrics whose ends dragged along the ground.

'Wrap yourself in this,' he said. 'Like this. Like this.'

One piece of cloth was red, very fine and brilliant, another was golden, like a veil, another was green.

Ariadne allowed his hands to wrap the fabrics around her, letting them fall in pleats, entirely covering her brown dress. She was still laughing. Alexander's enthusiasm was that of a man possessed.

'You would look beautiful…' he said at last. He was about to say more but stopped himself. Yes, she would look beautiful if clothed only in these fabrics, and nothing else. Just her naked body.

But he dared not say it. From one of the half-finished canvases her mother, Mrs Stevenson, under her ornate and elegant green hat, smiled at him, as if with a warning: 'Take care of my daughter.'

Alexander's face was red and perspiring, his brown hair tangled. The beating of his heart was so fast and strong that it must be audible through the walls of the room.

Ariadne got up from the rug and went close to him. The fabrics fell to the ground.

'Paint me however you want,' she said.

'I want to create a work unlike any I have ever painted before,' he admitted to her. 'Like the themes which used to inspire my teachers and which are all the rage in the artistic circles of the Royal Academy. A mythological painting, with characters from one of the ancient legends.'

She looked at him admiringly. It was the most exciting thing that had ever happened to her. In all the years she had lived in the warm and exotic country where she had grown up, she had never known a man with the openness, the energy and the force of Alexander.

'I've been waiting to find a model. A perfect face. And now I have it in front of me.'

Ariadne blushed, as if she had suddenly recognised what was happening between them, and felt the urgency in the eyes of the man she was alone with in the studio. But Alexander seemed so good, so sweet-natured, that she had never felt ill at ease with him. On the contrary, she sensed the presence of a special bond between them – like two children sharing a secret.

There were more afternoons when Alexander was alone with Ariadne in his studio. As he continued to paint the image of her face, his passion for her grew stronger still.

There were also more tea parties at the house of the Stevensons, and more dinners organised by Lady Hunter. Alexander began to feel completely integrated into this society to which he had never dreamed he could belong, among people who had already paid him a substantial amount of money. Some of his paintings were already hanging on the walls of the Morgans' house. And the portrait of Mr Stevenson was nearly finished.

But his relationship with James Stevenson had become tense. It was true they behaved cordially to each other while he was posing on the studio sofa and Alexander was painting. Sometimes they even chatted about inconsequential things, or drank tea or hot chocolate together. His face fascinated Alexander. He couldn't say whether this was because of his likeness to Ariadne or the way he half-closed his eyes, which gave him a mysterious and even menacing air. Or perhaps it had all started one afternoon when Margaret Stevenson had taken him aside while her husband was out of the way.

'Take care, Alexander,' she had said in a low voice, as if she scarcely dared to speak. 'My husband is an unpredictable and dangerous man. He adores his little daughter, and could not bear it if anything happened to her.'

Was this a warning?

But nothing *had* happened to her. Not yet…

Alexander had to admit that he loved Ariadne, that not a minute went by without him thinking of her. Every moment when he felt her close to him, he was almost in torment. And she? She had that freshness of youth which has just come into blossom, when malice is non-existent and feelings reveal themselves in the eyes without shame. And in those eyes he had seen tenderness, trust, admiration. Eyes which were identical to those of her father, yet totally different!

'The goddess Venus was born from the foam of the sea,' he told her one afternoon when they were alone in his studio. 'The most beautiful goddess on Olympus. A beauty among beauties. And her special province was the inspiring of love, the arousing of passion between gods and mortals. Love can be the most precious of gifts, or the most terrible punishment.'

Ariadne looked directly into his eyes, with a new expression on her face. Like that, she looked even more like Venus: all fire.

'Take off my dress,' she said suddenly, 'and cover me with those fabrics.'

Alexander could hardly breathe. There she stood, panting, blushing, with lips half-open. Like a child about to do something naughty. But also like a woman full of desire.

As if in a dream, he came up to her from behind and began to undo the buttons of her dress. His fingers moved clumsily over the silk of her bodice, but gradually he managed to uncover the white lace of her underwear, then the skin of her shoulders and arms.

When he saw her naked before him he could scarcely bear to fix his eyes on her, fearing she might disappear if he so much as looked at her. Or as if he were about to be punished for committing so grave a sin.

Such delicate skin. Such wonderful curves.

He could barely hold back. And Ariadne smiled at him mischievously, shamelessly.

'Alexander,' she said. 'Come here. Don't be afraid.'

How could he resist such an enchanting creature? He loved her. Yes, he loved her, with a passion that was almost painful. He wanted to possess her, to hold her in his arms, to press her body to his, and to explore every fold and corner. He wanted to kiss her firm breasts, to run his tongue over her thighs, to let her guide him until she gave herself to him completely.

He embraced her and began to kiss her, at first gently, then with all the passionate force which had been consuming him for the last few days.

'Afterwards I shall continue to paint you. You will shine with a different light after I have loved you.' These were his last words before they lay down together by the fire, two naked bodies each longing for the other.

He had no idea how much time had passed. He lay exhausted and happy at Ariadne's side, his breathing matching the rhythm of hers. Never had he had such an experience. At first timid and then provocative, Ariadne had taken him into an unknown world, making him feel reborn. But the reality was there. And suddenly he felt ashamed to have abused the innocence of this young girl, who perhaps confused admiration with love. He didn't want to hurt her, or to cause pain to her family.

If no one found out…

They dressed quickly, without saying a word. And they went back to work. But Alexander's inspiration had deserted him. There was nothing for him to capture in a painting when what he was feeling was so real, so alive that he could not turn it into something artificial, an image different from the woman he had in front of him. Ariadne was no longer Venus or Myrrha. She was simply Ariadne Stevenson, the woman he hoped would be his forever.

At last Margaret Stevenson came to collect her daughter. He watched the two of them leave, gossiping and laughing flirtatiously. Ariadne was once more elegantly dressed, with her cape and silk-ribboned hat – garments quite different from the fabrics which had clung to the roundness of her breasts and revealed the curves of her naked body.

It had been dark for some hours. The fire in the studio barely gave out any warmth. Alexander put down his brushes and went out of the room in which Ariadne's distinctive perfume still mingled with the smell of fresh paint. The pile of fabrics on the floor, on top of the rug, was the sole proof of what had happened between them.

4

It was the beginning of December. Preparations for Christmas were underway. On some days the sky was clear: dawn broke with the fields covered in a brilliant white veil. At other times the clouds formed a single grey mass, and the rain was incessant.

It was only a couple of days since that afternoon with Ariadne in his studio. Since then events seemed to have rushed ahead without pause. Even his usual visit to Lady Hunter's house had brought excellent news. Lord Robinson, already Alexander's partner in many a conversation, himself went to the house often, and this time he had told Alexander about a good friend of his who had contacts at the Fitzwilliam Museum in Cambridge. He had told this friend of Alexander's work, and the two of them had agreed to call in at the studio the following day. Apparently he was keen to contact new artists and to buy good paintings for the museum.

'A wonderful opportunity!' had been the unanimous view of those present. Katherine Morgan, enthusiastic as ever, burst out into demonstrations of delight. She had always known it! She knew Alexander would go far.

Alexander blushed. He still wasn't used to such praise. And immediately he thought of Ariadne. How happy she would be if she knew.

If he managed to get himself into a good financial situation, would he dare to ask her to marry him?

The night before the day of the visit, he could hardly sleep. He was kept awake by nerves and impatience, as his imagination dreamed of returning to London and moving there permanently, this time as an accomplished and recognised artist. Though he also knew that his talent could never equal that of Gabriel. That was something he couldn't aspire to.

Twice he left his room and went to his studio, oblivious of the cold air which blew in through the gaps in the window frames.

He looked critically at his own paintings. The unfinished portraits, the watercolours of the cathedral, Isolde with her medieval headdress… and the painting of Venus.

It will all turn out well, he thought, perhaps to convince himself that he had taken the right decision, and that falling in love with Ariadne would be the culmination of his desires and would not alter the promising future which his new friends saw as his destiny.

Before going back to his bedroom he looked longingly at the corner with the rug in front of the fireplace. It still held memories of Ariadne's seductive and passionate laughter, and of the moment of extraordinary pleasure which he had enjoyed with her.

Next morning he set to work energetically. Mrs Smith had come back from market with provisions for tea. She and her niece would take care of everything. After all, important gentlemen were expected, and that required some effort.

The fire had been lit since morning. The afternoon was cold and wet, and such daylight as there had been had already vanished.

Lewis Morgan, Lord Robinson, and his friend, a man by the name of Carpenter, arrived on time. Greetings were exchanged, and they all moved into the dining room. To Alexander the situation seemed not very different from those afternoons in the house of Lady Hunter, except that this time he was the host. The thought filled him with pride.

Mr Carpenter had a long grey beard and wore glasses. He looked altogether an agreeable person, with a very soft voice and an intelligent expression. He was clearly knowledgeable about art, and soon captivated Alexander with his account of the history of the Fitzwilliam Museum, which was now the pride of the city. It housed examples of the greatest masters of English painting from earlier centuries, as well as a splendid collection of antiquities – not the equal of the British Museum, perhaps, but important none the less.

Alexander was entranced. Cambridge. Close by, yet magical. He remembered having visited it first as a child long ago. The Gothic buildings and the medieval atmosphere of its streets and lawns brought back memories of the stories about chivalry which he used to read as a boy. This attraction for the beauty of the past had remained in his heart ever since, perhaps without his realising it.

Tea was relaxed and cordial. Lewis Morgan steered the conversation towards light-hearted topics. They talked about politics. There was no rush. A meeting of friends.

When the time came to visit his studio, the three guests were in the best of spirits and exceptionally keen to see the paintings, as if the viewing were an event of major significance and for their eyes only. Alexander had already described his style and technique, his apprenticeship in London, the conversations about Italian art with his masters. He wanted to make a good impression, and had surely done so. Yet he didn't know what Carpenter was hoping to find, nor what his tastes were. Very traditional? Very bold? Whether conservative or innovative, any expression of appreciation would be welcome.

Alexander ushered them in, full of anticipation. They approached the paintings cautiously, examining each figure detail by detail, brushstroke by brushstroke. Lord Robinson seemed satisfied. Lewis Morgan even made jokes.

'It takes a magnificent portraitist to get the best out of his model. I posed for hours, and I assure you it was worth it. My wife tells me she hasn't seen me looking so young and handsome since the day she met me.'

Mr Carpenter scrutinised the delicately coloured landscape with Ely Cathedral in the background. Then the medieval scene: Isolde madly in love with Tristan. Finally he went up to the huge canvas on which Venus was beginning to assume form.

'I'm not interested in portraits,' he said, 'but this is magnificent, although it's obviously unfinished. What is the subject?'

'It's a theme from classical mythology. The birth of Adonis, with the goddess Venus.'

'Finish it and bring it to me in Cambridge. If I like it I shall give you a good price, and we shall hang it in the Fitzwilliam.'

Lewis Morgan smiled at Alexander with conspiratorial satisfaction. For the brief moment the smile lasted, Alexander felt a sudden pang of doubt. Had he recognised Ariadne in the face on the canvas, even if it was no more than a sketch, albeit a suggestive one? Art expert that he was, his guest had sensed the force of the characters and admired the colour of the landscape; but he could have had no inkling of the passion Alexander had poured into the act of painting the woman who had been his model.

'I'm so grateful for your confidence in me,' he replied. 'Don't worry. You shall have the painting.'

'Something tells me I made the right choice. I know you won't let me down.'

After one last look at the paintings and drawings, the three men decided it was time to be on their way. Just before they left, Alexander had spoken to them about the art works of Dante Gabriel Rossetti and Edward Burne-Jones. The knowledge he had gained from his studies in London further enhanced the excellent impression that Alexander had made. Clearly his teachers' reputation had already extended beyond the capital, adding credibility and prestige to Alexander's own work.

Alone at last in the house, he reflected on everything that had happened in the last few years. It had all been for the best. He was lucky. His parents' house had gradually turned into a real home, the home of the new Alexander Knight that he had become. An artist.

Although in truth his surroundings hadn't changed much over the years, he had the feeling that they too were as new as his state of mind.

Next day he would go back to work. He would go to the Stevensons', and Ariadne would be there. He hoped to have the chance to tell her his good news. That the painting would fail to please the man who had commissioned it never occurred to him. His efforts would be rewarded. The painting would find its way to the Fitzwilliam.

5

LIFE IN ELY CONTINUED MORE OR LESS UNCHANGED. Winter had arrived in full force. You could sense that Christmas was very near.

Various of his new friends had invited Alexander to join them for the festivities: he really shouldn't be on his own at such a special time of the year. Although he himself didn't much mind solitude now that he had his work to do, in the end he had decided to accept the Morgans' invitation to spend Christmas Day with them. They were now his close friends, and he knew he would enjoy good cheer and merry company.

Twice he had returned to the Stevensons' house, and the adorable Ariadne had managed to evade her mother's watchful eye to be alone with him. They talked endlessly, and there was even time for a kiss. Each day she was more lovely.

Yet it was too soon to tell her family – especially her father – about his feelings for her. Though he couldn't explain it, Mr Stevenson sometimes made him afraid. That stare…

When he saw the two of them together, father and daughter, the resemblance struck him even more forcefully. Sometimes they even seemed to move in unison, as if driven by the same internal spring.

He had also observed in the father a peculiar, possessive attitude, which seemed to amuse his daughter. Shared glances, accidental touches of his hand and hers, all this gave Alexander a powerful sense of unease.

Margaret Stevenson was always charming. Nevertheless, now that he knew her better, Alexander could have sworn there was something forced about her cheerfulness, as if she were trying to convince herself that they were a happy and unified family, content to have found a new home in their native country after years spent abroad. But he had set aside those doubts about a family of which he hoped one day to form a part. He tried to concentrate on his work.

He prepared the canvas which he had brought with him and carefully selected some brushes. A few details remained to be added, but the portrait was almost finished.

Ariadne skipped playfully round him, oblivious of the effect she had on the beating of his heart and the colour of his cheeks. Then she went up close to her father as he held his pose and his stare, pinching him affectionately till he made an involuntary movement of his face and hands.

'You could paint a portrait of the two of us together,' she said, 'just Papa and me. That way it would be less serious. What do you think?' she added, turning to her father.

'Leave us alone, my dear. Mr Knight must finish his work.'

Ariadne pursed her lips as if she were annoyed. But immediately a smile returned to her face, and as she left the room she blew a kiss with her fingertips. Once more Alexander blushed. Was the kiss aimed at him or her father? And what of that rigid posture, those tense hands: were they part of the pose of the man in the armchair, or did they betray a powerful emotion only just kept under control?

For a few hours more he worked without pause, but he would probably need a little more time in his studio to put in the last touches. The whole family seemed delighted with the result.

That evening Alexander wanted to go back home early. There were some domestic matters which he had to sort out with Mrs Smith, and also some letters to write, not to mention Christmas cards – a new invention which had recently become popular.

At the door of the house a carriage was waiting to take him back to Ely. The horses seemed as impatient as he was.

The journey was slow. It had rained a lot, and the roads had turned into rivers of mud. Alexander was tired. He had worked with intense concentration and scrupulous attention to detail, mixing the colours with infinite care:

creamy rose for the cheeks, yellow and light brown for the hair, near-black for the jacket. In the background some objects in the room had also demanded his skill.

At long last he was satisfied. James Stevenson seemed to gaze out at him from the canvas, with that unsettling look which to Alexander – perhaps because he felt a certain degree of guilt – appeared to be menacing. But there could be no doubt that the portrait was good, or that the family would be proud of it.

The movement of the coach had made him drowsy. They must be almost there by now.

All of a sudden, when they were already in the town centre just a few yards from the house, the coach halted abruptly. The horses slipped in the mud. Alexander, taken unawares, was thrown against the coach door. Someone cried out.

Apparently a boy had almost fallen under the wheels of the coach. Why on earth had he run across the road at that moment? The coachman couldn't explain it.

Grumbling and swearing, the boy began bad-temperedly to retrieve the contents of the sack he had been carrying: some potatoes, some apples and a few onions, all now filthy with mud.

Still shaken from the sudden stopping of the coach, Alexander had now got down. His eyes met the boy's. He might have been sixteen or seventeen, but his face had the freshness of childhood. Under his clothes – which did not give the appearance of newness – his body was slender. His curly fair hair escaped from a cap which was too big for him.

He looked cross but seemed unhurt. Soon he would go on his way without paying much attention to the incident, indeed forgetting it altogether.

However, Alexander stood gazing at him, as if barely able to credit what he was seeing. That face, those curls…

The boy was what he was searching for. Adonis.

Into his mind came the image of his painting. The painting of his dreams. A painting whose subject was the figure of a mortal, a youth, almost a child, who captivated a goddess with his beauty.

He had his Venus: Ariadne. He had his Cinyras – Myrrha's father – with the face of James Stevenson. But for Adonis he had no model.

And now, suddenly, Adonis was in front of him.

'Hey!' he shouted, before the boy disappeared into the distance.

The youth turned round and then, intrigued, retraced his steps.

'Would you like to earn some money?'

He looked at Alexander cautiously, disbelievingly. 'Yes.'

'I'm a painter. I'm looking for a model. If you come to my house tomorrow and sit for me, I'll pay you well.'

Now the boy's smile was broad and trusting. After all, he had nothing to lose. 'All right, mister.'

'Mr Knight. I live in *The Willows*, second house on the left.'

The boy ran off, seemingly in a hurry. But Alexander was sure he would meet the appointment.

The coach accident had given him something he hadn't expected. What a coincidence.

He walked home in high spirits. He had no need of a coach: some fresh air would do him good.

He could barely wait to get back to work. The painting must be finished without delay. He had already been thinking about a date when he could go to Cambridge to visit Mr Carpenter. Maybe the week after Christmas would be a good moment, when the bustle of the festivities had died down.

*

After days of rain and sleet, at last dawn had broken with a clear sky. A timid sun gave colour to the countryside, which till then had been dyed grey. The pause in the bad winter weather seemed to have roused the inhabitants of Ely and put them in a good mood. All of a sudden they had gone out for a quiet stroll, to market or to visit neighbours. A constant stream of carriages drove from one end of the High Street to the other. Everywhere people from the countryside were coming and going with produce destined for Christmas parties.

The peals of the cathedral bells could be heard from far away.

Alexander had started work early. His new model was called Peter – though for Alexander he would always be Adonis. The boy had kept his word and presented himself on time. After eating eggs and tea with a healthy appetite, he had gone with Alexander to his studio.

The lad seemed obedient. He had sat where he was told and stayed quiet. He looked lost. He altered his posture or expression as Alexander instructed him.

Neither of them spoke. Alexander respected the privacy of this unknown boy who had come from goodness knows where; he hadn't asked him who his parents were or where he lived. Evidently he belonged to the humblest social class, and seemed used to following orders and working. As Alexander looked at him he felt a certain pity, conscious of his own good fortune in the way life had treated him well. Yet it was true that his own family had worked hard to earn its standing in society, his father in the shop which had enabled him to buy a small plot of land, his mother running the household and enjoying the new comforts of the age. In London, more than in Ely, he had become aware of social inequalities – the wealth and poverty which had both grown as a consequence of the recent industrialisation. He had witnessed the hard labour of the workers, the homeless. In the Working Men's College he had listened to theories about work for all, food for all. Surely some day, for Peter and boys like him, things were bound to change.

In any case, his beautiful and perfect face would be immortalised in a painting. Like Adonis, he would live forever.

As Alexander didn't want to tire him out, he asked him to come back another day. A couple more sessions would be enough.

The boy seemed reluctant to leave, but said nothing. Just a hesitant 'Thanks,' before he took his money and ran off down the street. He had the habit of running everywhere instead of walking. Alexander hoped he wouldn't have another accident, knocked down by one of the carts loaded with merchandise. Their drivers wouldn't be able to stop so easily.

After clearing up his painting materials Alexander decided to go out for a walk. It would do him good to stretch his legs and to take advantage of the unexpected morning sunshine.

He took the street which led straight down to the river. It was cold, but the kind of cold which invigorates. The brilliant sun melted the frost, turning it into tiny droplets which glinted on the grass like diamonds. The water of the canal reflected the azure sky: pure, clean, cloudless.

Other passers-by had obviously had the same idea as he had. Some boys were tossing stones into the water, trying to find out where the layer of ice was thinnest.

He waved to some people that he used to meet in the town hotel. His mind replayed the moments he had spent with Ariadne. Her laughter, the touch of her skin…

As he turned a corner, near the bridge, he thought he could make out in the distance two figures who seemed familiar. Two women, one young, the other older. The way they walked and moved. It was as if his thoughts had sprung into life: Ariadne and her mother.

They too had recognised him and hurried towards him. They had evidently gone out for a walk in their most comfortable and warmest clothes. Even so, there was an innate coquettishness about them, and Ariadne looked the most elegant woman he had ever known. Far more elegant than those London women who went to cocktail parties or the theatre escorted by their important husbands, women whom he used to contemplate with a certain longing in anticipation of one day finding the right wife for himself. Now that the cold had put colour in her cheeks, Ariadne's loveliness shone out all the more radiantly. He felt jealous that other men too could admire her.

Alexander blushed when he saw her smile of happiness.

'Alexander! What a surprise!' exclaimed her mother, as she took Alexander's hand affectionately. 'Out for a morning walk?'

'Yes, a stroll before lunch.' He was still a little taken aback by the unexpected meeting. 'And what brings you here, my dear ladies, so far from home?'

'We're going to spend Christmas at a friend's house.' This time it was Ariadne who replied, her voice full of the enthusiasm which she put into everything she did and said. 'What fun it will be to have a traditional English Christmas: turkey, Christmas pudding, games, sweets…'

'And your husband?' Alexander addressed his question to Margaret Stevenson. He was rather surprised to find the women unaccompanied.

She seemed to tremble slightly, but rapidly recovered her air of cheerful nonchalance. 'Oh, he's very well. Occupied as usual with his own affairs.'

The three of them set off walking together. How he longed to slip his hand into Ariadne's and to walk at her side, as if they were two lovers. But never mind. In any case his enjoyment was very special.

Ariadne's mother was interested in his paintings, and seemed sincerely glad to hear him describe his commission for the Fitzwilliam. One could tell that she was calm and relaxed. Perhaps because she was enjoying the fresh air. Or perhaps because she was far from her house, where things might not have been as they appeared to be.

After a while Mrs Stevenson lagged behind, as if she guessed her daughter's wish to be with Alexander. The two young people did not waste their opportunity. They walked very close to each other, so close that Alexander was sure she could sense the excitement she was arousing in him.

What a moment of happiness. He would have wished to bring time to a standstill, never to be separated from her again.

'I need to see you alone,' Ariadne suddenly whispered to him, waking him from his daydream. Her voice sounded nervous and urgent.

'What? What do you mean?' he replied in a low voice, startled at the idea that her mother might overhear them.

'It's important. I need to see you,' she repeated. 'Tomorrow night. At the station. Please—'

'But what's wrong? You're frightening me. Tomorrow is Christmas Eve.'

'It doesn't matter. It's my only chance. Before the holidays are over. I'll be in Ely till after New Year.'

Her smile was so sweet, so persuasive, that Alexander blocked all doubts from his mind. In any case it would be wonderful to see her again.

Would she want to visit his house again? Would they make love by the fireside?

Suddenly he became afraid. It would be better to do things in a different way. Step by step. To ask for her hand in marriage and to do so with the approval of her family. Such an enchanting girl did not deserve to be seduced as if she were a woman of easy virtue. She deserved a faithful, loving husband who would take care of her.

Alexander shivered. He buttoned his overcoat and pulled down his hat, trying to protect himself from the cold which, for some reason, seemed more intense, even though the sun was warmer now.

'All right, all right,' he replied, unable to hide a smile as he gazed into her eyes. 'I'll be there.'

'Whatever happens?'

'Whatever happens.'

Mrs Stevenson was catching them up. It was getting late, and they had to go home.

'Mr Knight,' she said, with a playful gleam in her eye, 'it has been a pleasure to see you again. I hope you will visit us at home – perhaps after the holidays?'

'The pleasure has been mine, to be in the company of two such beautiful ladies. And of course I shall be delighted to visit you.'

As Alexander watched Ariadne walk away, he felt an overwhelming need to run after her. But he remained still, and perplexed. Though he couldn't explain it, he had an intuition of something beyond his comprehension. Ariadne was in love with him, of that he was sure. And he saw that she was contented, as if that love were a fresh and stimulating experience in the process of her transition to womanhood. Yet her mother was a puzzle. She seemed to warm to the idea that he and her daughter should be mutually attracted. What was more, she seemed actually to want to foster that relationship. Perhaps she saw in him an ideal partner for her bold and bright Ariadne. A painter with a promising future. Even so, artists did not exactly have a reputation for fidelity in their love affairs. Rather, they were as fickle and capricious as their art.

This, he told himself, would not be true of *him.* In his heart he knew he could love Ariadne forever, that he could never even look at another woman. Elizabeth had disappeared entirely.

When he got home, he realised he was exhausted. The long walk, and the meeting with the Stevensons, had affected him physically and emotionally.

After eating the meat stew and potatoes prepared by the maid, he stayed in the dining room to read, sitting in the armchair next to the fireplace. It occurred to him that this was the chair his father used to sit in. He had almost forgotten that.

It was well into the afternoon when at last he decided to go to the studio to continue working. He couldn't waste time.

The familiar smell of paint brought back memories of the splendid studio in which Gabriel and Edward used to bring together their students, and where Alexander himself had taken his first steps in painting from life. Now, before his eyes, he saw the results of those classes: the lines of the bodies, the elements of the landscape, the curve of a neck – all of it the product of hours of hard apprenticeship.

The portrait of Ariadne's father was nearly complete. He sat in front of it and studied it with a critical eye, examining it for details which needed a final touch.

It was then that he noticed it. How strange. While painting, he hadn't been conscious of it, having been turning constantly from the man seated before him to the figure represented on the canvas. The face of the living man seemed to show no particular expression. It had the absent gaze and relaxed attitude of a man bored with spending too long in the same posture.

But now… It was as if his subconscious had reflected something unperceived by his senses. A threat in the eyes, a gleam of unrecognised evil. Without doubt, the man in the painting had a sinister air.

'But why?' he asked himself.

He walked away from the painting and then approached it again, convinced that his impression was mistaken. But it was not. The same look was there. And it seemed to be directed at him.

Alexander felt his stomach heaving. His hands began to sweat.

What if the family were annoyed? Even if Mr Stevenson really did make him feel uncomfortable, the last thing Alexander wanted was to cause pain or displeasure to the man's family.

He tried to relax, and to think.

Perhaps the explanation lay with Ariadne's mother, the delightful woman who had warned him against her husband. That warning, as well as the anxiety she displayed when she talked of her husband, must have affected Alexander profoundly.

He could paint over the portrait to cancel those features: to change the expression, to change that stare.

Beside the portrait stood the Adonis painting, in which the characters were timidly coming to life. And there, once again, was that same face in the image of Cinyras, the father who perpetrated an incestuous union from which was born that wonderful, almost divine creature.

Did Mr Stevenson hate him because he suspected him of trying to seduce his daughter? Was he protecting Ariadne's virtue?

The questions crowded in his brain. But suddenly a strange and malevolent certainty took hold of him.

The father was jealous, and the mother knew it. That was why she was afraid of him.

Alexander decided to act as if nothing had happened. He turned his eyes from the portrait, pretending it was all a product of his imagination. He got a little paint ready and prepared to work, focusing on mixing the colours and finding the exact hue to highlight the figure of Adonis against the dark background, an exuberant landscape which brought out his relationship with nature.

While he was painting, another thought struck Alexander, like a sudden ache.

Ariadne wanted to see him urgently. She had said it was important. But he hadn't taken it seriously enough: it was nothing more than the eagerness of a headstrong and passionate young woman who wanted to be alone with her lover. But now he realised that perhaps there was more to it: that something truly vital was distressing her.

Did she want to tell him that she was expecting a child?

He had to sit down to control his nausea.

He breathed deeply. If it was true, no matter. They would marry immediately. If need be, they would move far away. Maybe to London. There they would surely get help from Gabriel and his sister Christina, and from Edward and Georgiana. He would paint to commission, and could give his wife a good position in life.

His dreams mingled with his memories. Tomorrow. Tomorrow night, he would know.

6

ANXIETY HAD GRIPPED HIM THROUGHOUT THE DAY, and as the hours passed he could hardly remain still. Fear, excitement and worry succeeded each other with dizzying speed.

He would have liked to enjoy a quiet Christmas, painting and perhaps spending time with friends. His first Christmas at home since his return from London. However, recent events had swept him into a world of new emotions against which he was powerless to struggle.

Of course he wanted to be with Ariadne. But he now recognised that a relationship with her might be filled with difficulties, that it was more complicated than simply loving and being loved. His heart and his passion had carried him along a road that his reason told him might not be the right one.

He was afraid. Perhaps he was too young to face decisions which he had never before dreamed of taking. It was true that he had hoped one day to meet a woman, to marry, to have a family and be a good husband, as his father had been. But now, suddenly, he was unsure.

Twice he went to his studio and tried to work on the painting, but he could not. Behind him he could sense James Stevenson glaring at him. Those eyes – he himself had painted them, yet they seemed to have taken on a life of their own, to remind him of his guilt. That face – so like that of his beloved – seemed to be saying to him: 'Ariadne is mine. Do not dare to touch her.'

He had hardly eaten anything. Instead he spent some time getting things ready to take to the Morgans'. In different circumstances he would have relished the anticipation of a special day in the company of people with whom he got on well. Katherine and Lewis were generous hosts who would do everything to put him at his ease. Their daughter Susanna lacked the virtues and charms of Ariadne, but she was a placid and pleasant girl, easy to talk to.

Yet again and again Ariadne's words came back to his memory: 'I need to see you alone,' she had said. 'It's important.'

Would it be what he suspected? Or something to do with her father? He didn't want to contemplate other possibilities. Ariadne was certainly an impulsive and flirtatious woman. And she had a strong character, as he had come to realise. Perhaps she was just trying to evade the surveillance of her controlling father.

Alexander resolved to torture himself no longer. He would go to the station and wait for her. Never mind the dinner on Christmas Eve. Never mind the cold of the night. He would listen to what she had to say to him, and they would take their decisions together.

Early in the afternoon the postman arrived, in his characteristic and unmistakable red uniform. Among the numerous Christmas greetings Alexander found an unexpected surprise: a letter from Gabriel. At any other time, news from his old friend and teacher would have filled him with joy. Now, though, anything that Gabriel might have had to tell him was without interest, compared with his anxiety to discover what lay behind Ariadne's urgent plea.

He opened the letter mechanically and immediately recognised his friend's handwriting.

London seemed so far away now…

The letter was full of anecdotes about life in Oxford as they were decorating the walls of what would be the library of the Union. He, Edward Burne-Jones and William Morris were working hard but enjoying themselves enormously. The careers of all three seemed to be ascending ever higher. William had just exhibited a magnificent work, *Queen Guinevere*, and Gabriel was writing sonnets. 'I'm still dedicating myself to the beautiful art of poetry,' he wrote. 'The sonnets seem to compose themselves in my head of their own accord, without my being able to stop them.' Poetry was another of his passions. It was incredible that he found time to do so much.

When the time came to go out he put on his warmest clothes in preparation for combat with the intense cold, the wind and the incessant rain. In this weather the walk to the station would take him much longer than usual.

The maid was surprised to see him leaving the house at such a late hour. But he gave no explanation.

The streets were empty. Not many people would venture out on a night like that, unless they had a very good reason.

The station was equally deserted. Perhaps no train was due at that hour. The stationmaster, asleep in his little office, was the only living soul in the neighbourhood.

Of Ariadne, of course, there was no sign.

Alexander tried to take shelter as best he could. The wind blew gusts of icy water which clouded his vision and soaked his lips. With one hand he held on to his hat; with the other he took out his pocket watch from his overcoat. Ten o'clock. Ariadne should be there. But how was a young woman to leave her house in such weather? Her mother would surely prevent it. And to slip out unseen? Very unlikely.

Minutes turned into hours. He could barely feel his feet, even though he had been walking up and down the platform to try to get warm.

No. Ariadne would not come.

Suddenly, he felt despair. What could he do? He *must* see her. He could not delay it until after Christmas. That was too long to wait.

He left the platform and began to walk beside the railway tracks. A little way in that direction there was the bridge over the river. Perhaps she was waiting for him further off...

His feet sank into the mud. He didn't even know if

he was following a path or if he was lost in the middle of a field. But no: there to his right the tracks continued, illuminated by a distant gas lamp, as if they had been polished by the rain.

I ought to go home, he thought. It's madness to go on like this.

By now the darkness was complete. He carried on walking next to the tracks. His feet got caught up in the undergrowth, but for a while he managed not to fall. It was impossible that Ariadne had come as far as this.

He was approaching the bridge – he guessed it rather than seeing it.

It all happened in an instant, without him realising what or who it was that was approaching him. A shadow among shadows.

'Ariadne?' he managed to say, with a note of relief and hope in his voice.

Then he felt himself being violently pushed. He lost his balance, fell and rolled over the wooden sleepers.

He tried to get up but fell once more. There was blood on his face and hands. His arm hurt.

The last thing he saw was a huge dark mass, like an iron monster screeching towards him.

Cambridge

The present day

1

It was Sunday. Anna Carter had had a visit from Emma. Sad and distracted, Emma couldn't disguise the fact that something was wrong.

It had been a sudden decision to go to see her mother. But she didn't know what she was hoping to find there. Support? Consolation? Yet she realised that being with her mother wasn't going to be much help. Probably what she actually wanted was to get out of Cambridge, as if being physically distant from her house and her domestic routine would also keep away the doubts and worries which assailed her.

But even in London she was incapable of thinking clearly. She had a meal, just about followed a trivial conversation, and managed twice to resist telling her mother about what was happening.

But it would have been pointless to tell her, and Emma knew it. Anna would have become over-anxious and tried to convince her to move from Cambridge and come back to live with her. The same old story.

It had been only two days since she had broken up with Paul, and she had already entirely deleted him from her life. He had disappeared without a trace. In his place there was Julian. But a Julian who continued to be nothing more than a companion in her torment, which consisted in going incessantly to the museum, the two of them possessed by a longing for something unknown and unattainable.

She and Julian talked, went for meals together, and spent their afternoons in the library. There Emma devoted herself to reading about nineteenth-century English artists, hoping to come across a new fact or a new reference – this time it wasn't for her thesis, but to uncover a mystery in her own life.

Her sleepless nights too were filled with thoughts of Julian. She missed his company. She imagined what he would be like in bed. Tender, passionate... She was sure that making love with him would be perfect. Even so, nothing had happened between them yet, and she didn't know whether anything *would* happen. Sometimes she wondered whether she was capable of attracting him, of conquering him. But what did she know about men? She knew how she had met Paul, in her youthful inexperience, and had let herself be drawn into a relationship which seemed natural and inevitable. Paul was young, like she was, and like the other boys she had had brief relationships with. But Julian was a mature man, with surely a number of experiences in his past. She knew it wasn't going to be so simple.

When it was nearly time for Emma to leave to catch the train back to Cambridge, her mother gave her a worried, almost tearful look.

'Something's wrong with you. I know it,' she said, doubtless choosing her words carefully so as not to drive away her unresponsive daughter. 'You've tried to hide it, but I know you well. I know I've made mistakes with you, but believe me, I'm on your side.'

Emma avoided her look, whether out of fear or shame. In any case, how could she even begin to tell her that she was having visions of another era?

'Thanks, Mum. I'll be fine. It's nothing more than a bad patch I'm going through, you know…'

Emma left it at that, knowing full well that her mother would assume it was a matter of boyfriend problems. Although she hadn't told her much about Paul, Anna did know about their relationship. And it was true she had broken up with Paul. But that wasn't the thing that was causing her pain. The break-up had been the result of everything else.

Eventually they said their goodbyes. Soon Emma was alone on her way back home, on a train packed with passengers. Her idea of travelling to London had been so sudden that she hadn't even told Mary about it. In fact when she left, at an hour very early for a Sunday, Mary had still been asleep.

Emma shut her eyes for a while, trying to block out the noise around her: young people returning to university after a weekend away, families with children… At least, she thought, they all belonged to the twenty-first century.

She was longing to get back home. Her flat, Mary's laughter, her companions – all this would give her the sense of security which she needed. Or maybe what she *really* longed for was to see Julian, and to be with him. Although he brought her more uneasiness and uncertainty, he had become the most important person in her life.

She took her mobile out of her bag and keyed in his number. She wasn't sure what to say to him, but she wanted to hear his voice.

'Emma, where are you?' was his response from the other end of the line.

'On the train from London. I'll be back in half an hour. Are you OK?'

'Yes, I'm fine. Do you want me to meet you?'

'Don't bother if it's too late—'

'I'll be there, and I'll take you home.'

Sometimes she wondered how Julian could bear the situation. She knew he ought to return to his work and that his clients were demanding to see him. Even so, here he still was in Cambridge, lodging in a small hotel on the outskirts, putting up with the inconveniences of being away from home. She also wondered if his reason for staying had something to do with her. The thought brought a lump to her throat.

She got off the train, her cheeks red and her heart beating very fast. Not even the winter chill could cool the warmth which had seized her body.

There he was. Smiling. Almost frozen with cold.

'Let's get a taxi,' he said.

They looked at each other for a few seconds, which seemed like hours. Very near to him in the taxi, Emma longed to feel him so close that she could recognise the touch of his overcoat and the warmth of his body next to hers.

He had been avoiding her eyes now. He knew she had broken up with Paul, but he had said nothing, perhaps realising the contradictory feelings that had invaded her heart.

'Are you well?' he asked. She knew what he was referring to.

No, she had had no more visions or dreams. But that meant nothing. There was still a puzzle that she was determined to resolve.

'Did you go to the museum today?' This time it was Emma who asked the question.

'Yes. And I missed you.'

'The answer must be there, but we don't know what it is or when we shall find it. I want to go on researching.'

'Do you think we're going to have some kind of "revelation"? But that's absurd.'

The taxi driver stopped outside the block of flats where Emma lived. If he wondered at any point what sort of conversation his two passengers were having, he made no comment about it. After all, there were plenty of lunatics on the loose in the world.

Emma and Julian parted, without any physical contact between them, but with their eyes veiled with longing, as if they wanted to tell each other: 'I'd like to stay with you.'

'See you tomorrow,' was all they said.

Mary wasn't in. When Alice saw Emma arrive, she told her that Mary had gone out, then shut herself in her room on the pretext that she had work to do.

Emma was glad to be alone. She needed time to order her thoughts.

Her books were on the table where she had left them the previous night. Notes and other documents relating to her thesis were piled up alongside them.

There too was the information about the painter who interested her now, though she hadn't managed to find out any more about him. She was still anxiously waiting for the photocopies which her tutor had promised her, even if she realised they might be no more than biographical data or artistic studies of just one more nineteenth-century painter. Even so, they were her only hope. She put more faith in them than she did in a possible diagnosis by a psychiatrist.

She switched on her computer and started a new internet search: the Fitzwilliam Museum.

Here was the webpage about its history and foundation. She checked the date: 1845. Then she moved on to read about the permanent collections and the most recent exhibitions. But there was nothing she didn't know, nothing she hadn't read already. What was she hoping to find? She had no idea.

When at last she went to bed exhausted, she thought of Julian. She couldn't imagine life without him. Was this love? If it was, it was certainly something she hadn't experienced before. Not even with Paul. It went far beyond sex.

She wanted Julian for herself alone. If only they could be together…

An hour had passed when she heard the sound of the front door. Mary. Emma shut her eyes. She wanted her friend to think she was asleep. She didn't have the strength for a conversation over a bottle of wine.

She slept for a few minutes and woke up with a start, as if from lack of air. In her subconscious she had sensed a strong smell which filled her lungs and prevented her from breathing: a smell of paint.

2

THE MUSEUM WAS ALMOST EMPTY. THE ATTENDANTS greeted them like two old friends, no longer finding it strange to see them every day. A professor and his tutee, perhaps. Or two students, one of them not so young, preparing their end-of-term assignments.

They sat next to each other in the usual gallery, surrounded by the usual paintings. Nothing seemed to have changed. Even their anxiety was the same, their fear of seeing once more those visions of the past while being powerless to avoid them. What would happen if those visions returned?

'I was terrified of being unable to go out into the street again,' Emma confessed in a whisper. 'That's why I went to London. I thought that, whatever it is that's happening to me, at least it wouldn't reach me there.'

'I couldn't bear it for anything to happen to you,' he replied. 'It doesn't matter what happens to *me*; but I don't want you to suffer any more.'

'But what can we do? How can we escape it? If we don't know the cause, we can't find the cure.'

Julian nodded pensively. She could read the worry in his eyes. And in the midst of her own distress, Emma felt a wave of tenderness for this man, still a stranger, who had now come to form a part of her life.

It was curious that she could feel herself to be almost happy at a moment when the whole of her previous existence seemed to be disintegrating.

As always, the time passed imperceptibly. Visitors to the gallery came and went. Murmured conversations rose and fell.

And then, suddenly, a young man appeared in the room. He stopped for a moment and looked around, then went into the next room, then returned. He moved quickly and behaved strangely, as if running away from someone.

Emma stood up. The young man seemed to notice her presence and looked directly at her.

Then Emma became very frightened. The young man's face bore an expression of such horror, such uncontainable terror, as if he had witnessed some dreadful event and was seeking help.

He was slim, very good-looking, and well dressed. To judge by his age he might have been a first-year student, or even still at school.

Julian took Emma's arm gently, and they made as if to leave. But the boy stood in front of them, blocking their way.

'Wait!' he said, in a tone of desperation. 'Where am I? What am I doing here?'

His eyes were red, as if he had been crying. His lips were trembling.

Emma tried to move away from him. A drunk, she thought. Or an addict. Though he didn't look like either.

'Please,' he begged them, realising now that if he didn't control himself they would hurry away from him. 'I just want someone to explain to me what's happening here. You,' he said to Julian, 'I saw you here yesterday.'

Emma began to feel seriously ill at ease, as if she had a presentiment of what was about to happen, something deeply unpleasant.

The young man abandoned his aggressive attitude and went to sit down on one of the benches, burying his face in his hands. He gave the impression of someone wretchedly unfortunate, at the mercy of a pain whose intensity none but he could know.

'I'm sorry,' he said, when he raised his head. 'I'm sorry I frightened you. But I'm so confused… Nothing like this has ever happened to me before.'

Emma and Julian looked at each other for an instant, and then turned to the boy. No words were needed for them to comprehend that this formed part of the extraordinary events which had begun some weeks ago, and which continued to convulse every moment of their lives.

This young man's uncertainty, distress and desperation recalled to them their own first experience in the museum, when they understood neither the how nor the why of their presence there.

'Listen,' said Julian softly, choosing his words with care, 'this is the Fitzwilliam Museum, the exhibition of nineteenth-century painting.'

'I can see that. I'm not stupid. But I've never had the slightest interest in art. I came here, but I don't know why. For days now I've been having peculiar dreams, and when I woke up today the only thing I wanted to do was to come to this museum.'

Emma felt what seemed like an electric shock surging through her body. Someone else. How many others might there be? Was this sickness contagious? Or maybe this gallery produced an astonishing effect on those who stood within it.

Emma and Julian began to speak, almost at the same time. Uncertain at first, but then sure they were doing the right thing. Their own story would help the young man, if not to understand his situation, at least to know he was not alone.

'My name is Lucas,' he said, standing up and shaking Julian's hand. Then he sat down and once more hid his head in his hands.

Emma and Julian waited, respecting his silence.

When he looked up, his expression had changed. He had incredibly blue eyes, the most notable feature of a face which in other circumstances would have seemed beautiful, delicate, almost feminine.

'Are you telling me that for weeks the same has been happening to you?' His smile was sorrowful now, as if he were imagining how much suffering was still in store for him.

'Don't worry. You get used to it,' observed Julian ironically.

They looked at each other disbelievingly. Then they looked at the paintings which surrounded them. There was no explanation. Or at least, *they* had no explanation.

Emma told him of her visit to the hospital. It wasn't the kind of thing she would have related to a complete stranger, but perhaps this boy had a clue which would help them penetrate the mystery.

'And is it true you sometimes think you're in another era?' Lucas went on. 'In my dreams I couldn't locate myself very well. I don't understand any of this. This is my first year at Cambridge and I'm reading Economics.' He added with a note of pride, 'One day I'm going to work in my father's company.'

For a moment Emma felt pity for him: very good-looking, certainly from a good family, with a brilliant future ahead of him. But he also seemed very vulnerable. He surely didn't deserve this distress. But then, nor did she or Julian. The strange "sickness" had already transformed many aspects of her life: it had taken Paul away from her, it kept her from working on her thesis, and it had aroused emotions which now she could not control.

With complete naturalness Emma rested her hand on Julian's arm. The two of them walked slowly and hesitantly towards the exit. Lucas followed them with his eyes but remained seated in the middle of the gallery, absorbed in his own thoughts.

When they were out of the museum, Emma felt lost. Outside those walls, life was difficult and insecure. Outside those walls, Julian belonged to a world she didn't know, with a job, friends and a home. Only in the museum were they really together. And she realised that she needed him more and more…

They had a quick bite to eat in the library café. They said nothing, still stunned by the scene they had witnessed a few minutes earlier.

What connected them with this young student? Why did this illness – if you could call it that – affect all three of them?

Questions without answers.

Emma wanted to carry on reading books and articles, in search of more information about the life and work of Knight. Julian went along with her. He had nothing else to do.

As always happened while she was working, Emma became oblivious of everything else. As she sat at a table in the library with Julian beside her, she immediately felt relaxed and contented, as if she had recovered something of her previous life as a student, when an assignment successfully completed filled her with satisfaction.

She pored over page after page which took her from Rossetti to Millais, from Burne-Jones to Morris. She took notes on things she already knew. But three times she came across the name of Knight, as well as another reference to the article she was waiting for. Nothing more.

Suddenly she felt a bit dizzy. It wasn't surprising: all that accumulated exhaustion…

She raised her head from the books and looked behind her. The room was completely transformed. There was scarcely any light now, and the walls were panelled in wood right up to the ceiling. Huge volumes were piled up on the tables. There were no laptops now, nor electric lights. Two serious-looking men, dressed from head to foot in black, had their heads buried in books.

She must have cried out, because the next things she saw were the astonished faces of two girls working at tables in the row in front of her, and Julian's hand resting on hers.

'Let's get out of here,' he whispered to her urgently, realising that something had happened.

Emma followed him towards the exit, as if sleepwalking, still midway between the past and the present. The books lay open on the table, abandoned.

'It's probably because I'm tired,' was the excuse she made when they got out into the street. She tried to summon up a smile for Julian, who couldn't disguise his agitation.

'Exactly the same happened to me yesterday,' he confessed, 'but I didn't want to frighten you.'

'Maybe we should have had a longer talk to Lucas, to look for a connection between the three of us.'

'Always supposing there *are* just the three of us…'

Emma nodded, in a state of bewilderment.

'If this was a science fiction film, an extraterrestrial force would have seized control of the planet,' said Julian with a smile. Emma couldn't tell whether he meant it or whether he was just trying to cheer her up. In any case it was obvious that Julian was attempting to handle the situation with humour and irony. Yet at the same time he was impotent in the face of something beyond his comprehension and beyond his capacity to resist it, and was behaving like a sick man written off by the doctors as a hopeless case.

Outside it was already night. The days were getting shorter, and the obscurity suited their state of mind. On some trees and in the streets and shop windows, the Christmas decorations evoked the approaching season. Time was passing so quickly…

They walked in silence, still fearful and disturbed. Once again, Julian accompanied her to her home.

How Emma longed to ask him to come up to her room and stay with her. But she didn't dare to. Nor did he expect it. Circumstances prevented them from behaving like a man and a woman who didn't mind if their relationship developed from friendship into something more serious.

But it was hard for her to hold herself back.

And Julian? In spite of the age difference, his instinct was driving him towards her. But something stopped him. What could they have said to each other? How could they become a normal couple?

One day, thought Emma, it will all sort itself out.

3

THE SEDATIVE PRESCRIBED BY THE DOCTOR HAD done her no good. Emma still couldn't get to sleep. Fatigue compounded her restlessness, and even took away her appetite.

She had got up at about seven, tired of tossing and turning in a bed where she knew she would find no peace, and where nightmares mingled with her longing to be with Julian.

Even before she had breakfast, she was already at the computer. She began by looking at the webpage of the Fitzwilliam Museum, even though she knew by heart what she would find there. Then she looked up the Royal Academy of Art in London, searching for information about Alexander Knight. If he had been a member of the Pre-Raphaelite Brotherhood, he must have worked in London.

But nothing there either.

Then the computer alerted her that she had a new email message waiting. She opened it: it was from her tutor. Obviously he started work early too. It was a brief message to tell her that the photocopies and photos he had ordered had arrived.

Emma smiled. At last something that might lead her somewhere. Where, she wasn't at all sure, but she trusted blindly in her intuition, which she hadn't lost in spite of the chaos in her mind.

She decided that now wasn't the time to go on with her internet search: this was much more important than anything she could find online.

A quick cup of tea in the kitchen cleared her head. She needed to feel well, or at least well enough to cope with a day filled with mysteries and perhaps fresh news.

Mary had just got up.

'You look bad,' she said. Her reproachful look seemed to say: 'You're avoiding me, and I don't like it; but I'm still your friend.'

'I know,' Emma replied, feeling momentary guilt. 'Sorry I haven't spoken to you. Maybe tonight. But now I'm in a hurry.'

Mary watched her leave. She missed Emma as she used to be – a serious and thoughtful companion, eager to finish her thesis, and in love with a marvellous guy. A friend she could trust and have good times with.

Emma hesitated between making directly for the university or going to her usual rendezvous at the museum.

When she was already on her way to the university, she realised that the museum was actually the place she most longed to be. It was a completely irrational idea

– she was consumed by impatience to read the article which had arrived – but she couldn't fight it. Julian would be there. Besides that, she was intrigued to find out if Lucas had returned. It would be extraordinary if there was anyone else in the same situation.

The museum was still closed. In her hurry she had forgotten that it was still more than half an hour till opening time. She crossed the road and walked a few yards. There was a café a bit further down the street; a cup of coffee would do her good.

At that time of the day the place was full. She waited her turn in the queue at the counter behind a group of Chinese girls, then, cup in hand, looked around for a seat. Her eyes met those of a young man sitting by the window.

Lucas.

Emma was unsure whether to approach him directly. This café wasn't like the museum. Here they were just two ordinary people, two students having breakfast.

But the boy's attitude hadn't changed. He looked nervous and frightened.

'What are you doing here?' he asked Emma sharply when he recognised her.

'The same as you, I imagine,' she replied. 'The museum is shut.'

'And the other man?'

Presumably he meant Julian.

Emma sat opposite him. Lucas looked around fearfully as if expecting to see someone he didn't want to meet. It was the look of a disturbed individual who believes he has enemies everywhere. Then he rubbed his eyes with the back of his hand.

'I don't even know where I am,' he admitted. 'It's like I'm living in a dream.'

Emma nodded. She knew the symptoms well.

'Tell me something. Have you seen a painting in your nightmares? A painting signed A. R. K.?'

He thought for a while. Maybe he hadn't heard Emma's question?

'How is it possible?' he said, talking to himself rather than to the woman sitting opposite him. 'Yes, I've seen a painting. Sometimes more than one. A room full of paintings. And there's something which makes me feel really uncomfortable. It's like I'm going to die.'

Poor lad, thought Emma. And her next thought was that there had to be a reason for all these visions and nightmares.

Lucas got up suddenly. 'Come on, we *must* go to the museum.'

Emma finished her coffee and followed him into the street. He was walking so quickly that she could barely catch up with him.

When they climbed the great staircase leading up from the entrance they met Julian, wearing a dark blue windcheater and a striped scarf which covered part of his face. They all walked to the gallery that housed the Victorian paintings.

They were like three people in a trance, or from another world. Nothing in their surroundings had any meaning. Julian, perhaps, had allowed himself to be carried away by the situation without offering resistance, but Emma was still struggling to understand, convinced that with understanding would come the power to destroy the strange force which held them prisoner.

Emma gazed at Lucas. So young; hardly more than a child. And so handsome…

The idea that Mary would have loved to meet him made Emma smile.

Utterly detached from the other occasional visitors to the gallery, they concentrated on viewing the paintings.

Once more Burne-Jones's angels, the gentle green hills beside the English coastline.

'What have I got to do with this museum?' asked Lucas, with the same desperation as he had shown the day before. 'I hadn't been here before, but now it seems familiar to me. And I'm frightened to go home to sleep because I know something terrible might happen to me.'

'The initials. Are you sure you've seen them in the painting?'

'Yes, I think so. What do they mean?'

Emma now told him about the existence of a painter whose name corresponded to the initials. She also mentioned the message she'd received, and the photocopies waiting for her in her tutor's office.

'It may be that our visions correspond to reality,' she said. 'The painting might be by a nineteenth-century artist called Knight. My theory is that if we can find out more about him and his works we may get a clue to our own situation.'

Lucas looked at her, unconvinced. All this was nonsense. But for Julian, as for Emma, it offered a glimmer of hope. Improbable as it was, the mere fact of following this lead provided the possibility of an explanation, and they should cling on to it with all their strength. Without it, they were heading for the deepest frustration.

'We have to find out who this painter was, and what was the link between him and the museum. There must have been one.'

'Is there no painting by him in this gallery?'

Lucas scrutinised the canvases. By now the figures in them had become old friends. Their clothes, and the landscape behind them, no longer belonged to a remote past, but lived on in the present – his present.

Emma's agitation took more and more complete control of her, and she had no notion of how to cope.

'I have to go to the university,' she announced at last. 'Will the two of you come with me?'

She looked at Julian with the expression of yearning which he was used to. It aroused conflicting emotions in him.

Lucas shuddered. Go where? He had no idea.

'I think I prefer to stay here. I don't know what all this is about, but I don't like it.'

Julian shrugged and went up to Emma. It was clear that any movement cost him an enormous effort, and that with the part of his mind that was still sound he was trying to control those other strange and irrational impulses. At the same time this saner self told him that his duty was to protect and support Emma.

They left the museum like people abandoning a place of safety to confront the unknown, without knowing what the outside world had in store for them.

The History of Art Department was quite close by, but the weather was bitterly cold and the walk felt endless.

They were glad of the warmth inside the building when Emma went to her tutor's office. Julian promised to wait for her outside.

Her meeting didn't last long. Professor Ford apologised for not having more time to spare, but it was his tutorial hour and he was expecting some pupils to come to discuss their end-of-term essays. Maybe they could meet another day for a coffee? Emma thanked him, but the truth was that she didn't much mind not prolonging their conversation. The only thing she wanted this time was to look at the photocopies contained in a brown envelope with her name on it.

So excited was she that her hands were trembling as she said goodbye to her tutor, thanking him again for the trouble he had taken. There would be time for a chat another day.

Once outside the office she opened the envelope. Julian came up to look at it with her but said nothing, realising the impatience which was consuming her. They were in a small room with two seats next to the corridor. Taking no notice of the students who came and went, they set about leafing through the photocopies.

The title of the article was "The Pre-Raphaelite Aesthetic". In it there did indeed appear the name

"Alexander R. Knight", accompanied by a short biography. Born in Ely in Cambridgeshire, he had studied art in London. His speciality had been portraits. He had in fact never belonged to the Pre-Raphaelite Brotherhood, and his work was not well known. He had died very young, probably – like other Romantic artists – a victim of his own excesses.

As she read, Emma felt the anguish of her nightmares becoming more and more real. Even so, she had to admit that the information in the article told her nothing. Aside from the detail that the painter came from the neighbourhood of Cambridge, the rest of it seemed insignificant. Since his career had been so brief, he had evidently soon been forgotten.

Conscious of Julian looking over her shoulder, she continued to turn the pages till she came to two photographs of what seemed to be a painting set in the medieval period: a woman wearing a long blue robe and white headdress was standing in front of a background featuring some stained-glass windows and stone arches. To one side were represented some tapestries, which to Emma's eyes resembled those by William Morris.

But there was something else, something they certainly weren't expecting. They both recognised it at the same instant: the face of the woman in the painting bore an extraordinary resemblance to the face of Emma.

Those cold academic facts in the article now seemed unimportant. Was this an amazing coincidence? If not, what did it mean?

'Is it me?' whispered Emma, having almost lost the strength to speak. 'It can't be so; it just can't be.'

Julian didn't dare to say anything; he was as shaken as she was. The voices of students going from one lecture to another lost themselves in the distance.

'Forget it,' he replied at last, as if he had changed his mind. 'Don't worry. It has nothing to do with you.'

'I want to go home.' She looked as if she was going to faint.

They went out of the building. An icy wind was blowing as they crossed one of the bridges over the river; it brought Emma back to life and restored her energy. Colour had come back to her cheeks.

Julian walked beside her, as if wanting to keep the cold from her, and at the same time needing her physical presence.

He was close enough to feel the agitation of her breathing as she walked, and the rapid movement of her whole body.

'We don't know who that woman was,' panted Emma, 'but the Pre-Raphaelites used to paint their wives and their mistresses. Rossetti painted Morris's wife, Burne-Jones painted his lover Maria Zambaco…'

In the midst of her bewilderment, Emma had once again become the researcher she had always been: she habitually pursued any fragment of information which might lead her to a conclusion, and corroborated her ideas through study and analysis. This time, though, she felt that what was at stake wasn't a doctoral thesis, an article, or a lecture, but her very self and her bizarre state of mind. What she sensed was that this physical resemblance was no mere coincidence: rather, it was one more in the chain of inexplicable events in which she was enveloped.

They came to the front door almost automatically and went inside in the same condition. For the first time it seemed natural that Julian should go up with her to her room. There was no reason to say goodbye in the street, and neither of them said a word.

Mary was in the flat, finishing getting ready to go to work. The television was on, but there was nobody to listen to the pair of presenters rounding off their morning programme of interviews. Mary was obviously surprised when she saw her friend come in accompanied by a man. Emma realised she couldn't ignore Mary, so she greeted her and made a brief and quick introduction:

'Mary, this is Julian. Julian, my flatmate Mary.'

The two of them went straight to her room, leaving Mary as confused as she was curious.

Emma put the photocopies on the table and switched on her laptop. Julian couldn't help feeling a little uncomfortable at this intimacy with Emma. Her presence was so intense in the room: her clothes on a chair, her books piled on the shelves, her more-or-less-made bed, and a slight scent of the perfume she always wore. In the end he sat in silence on the edge of the bed, as if nervous about invading a forbidden territory.

After reading the article more carefully, Emma made some notes: the date of the painting, 1858; the years when Knight studied in London; the Pre-Raphaelite influence on his work, which could be seen in his use of colour and representations of the human figure. But there was nothing about that model, or about any woman he might have had a relationship with.

'We need to find out her identity,' said Emma, in a tone of desperation.

They seemed to have reached a dead end. The internet told them nothing they didn't know already. Nor did the numerous books that Emma had worked with for her thesis. Julian moved closer to her, looking over her shoulder at the computer screen.

'I don't do the kind of research that you do,' he said, 'but I know various artists who have exhibited in my gallery, and how they work. Our painter must have had several models, and probably worked on a number of canvases at the same time. If we knew something about those other paintings and could compare them…'

Emma shook her head. It might be an almost impossible task to trace those other paintings if they had gone to auction and been bought by individuals. But an idea began to form in her head. Knight had studied in London. In those years, after the first Pre-Raphaelite Brotherhood had disbanded, some artists had pupils and worked as a group. Now that painting of the medieval woman reminded Emma strongly of the representations of King Arthur which held such a fascination for Rossetti, Burne-Jones and Morris.

'Maybe he studied with them, even if later he followed his own direction in his career. There might have been letters between them—'

'But where could we search for them?'

'The British Library. Or perhaps in contemporary archives in the place where he lived. Assuming they exist...'

She looked at Julian and noticed the intensity of his expression. In his eyes there was a special brilliance which made her tremble. They were so close, just the two of them alone in her room. A few seconds passed, which seemed like hours; Emma waited longingly, without quite knowing for what. Then, abruptly, Julian moved back and away from her, breaking the tension of the moment. What might have happened, they would never know.

'I still don't see what connection there is between this story and us, but it doesn't matter. Let's keep on going,' he said, before getting up and making as if to leave the room. He needed air.

4

ONLY TWO DAYS HAD PASSED SINCE SHE HAD GONE to Professor Ford's office, but already some things had changed. Two days in which the hours they had spent in the museum had been a time for discussion, reflection, analysis and evaluation of what they now knew about this figure from the past, who seemed so mysteriously to be linked with their own lives.

Lucas, though, was unconvinced.

'I'm diabetic,' he had told them. 'I've made an appointment with my doctor to try and find out if what's happening to me has something to do with my medical condition.'

If Julian was also unconvinced, he disguised it well. In reality Emma was the only one who held on to a kind of optimism, or at least forced herself to, persuading herself that they were on the right track.

She had no faith any more in a clinical explanation, whether neurological or psychiatric, associated with a possible brain malfunction. How could three people have the same medical problem in the same place and at the same time? No, there must be another, external cause – however strange it might be – a cause wholly unconnected with the individual functioning of their bodies.

At the cost of a tremendous effort she had managed to travel to London again, to spend an afternoon alone in the British Library. Neither of the other two felt up to accompanying her, and she hadn't insisted. If she missed Julian, she hadn't shown it.

She returned to Cambridge weighed down with photocopies and with a whirlwind of ideas seething in her brain. They were all peculiar ideas, difficult to accept. But she was satisfied because some of the data corroborated her theories.

It appeared that Alexander Knight had been an art student in the Working Men's College in London, founded by the socialists in 1854. Some of the Pre-Raphaelite artists had given painting classes there. Most of Knight's work was now unknown, but he had doubtless followed in the footsteps of his teachers.

It wasn't clear why he hadn't pursued his career in London like the other artists of the group, moving instead to the city of Ely, where he concentrated on painting portraits. Maybe the reason had to do with family matters, thought Emma, trying to penetrate the painter's emotions and to imagine his personal and artistic development. Family matters which had stopped him from attaining fame in the capital. Something that didn't surprise her was the fact that he had died so young. It was common enough in those days that poets and artists were driven to suicide by their excesses or their emotional involvements. Lives cut short by desperation, love, or the longing for success. Lives in which artistic inspiration had carried them from the most exultant creative euphoria to the deepest despair.

Emma went straight back home. It was late, and she was physically and emotionally drained. She yearned for the company of someone to whom she could talk and open her heart, knowing they would understand. But she was aware that in the last few days she had rejected any friendly contact so as to focus on her obsession – an obsession which was partly with Julian and partly with her research into the past. Perhaps she was making a mistake in breaking with everything which had hitherto had importance in her life.

Mary was in her room, working at the computer.

Emma approached her door.

'No need to hide or to walk on tiptoe,' was Mary's comment from the other side of the door. 'I heard you arriving. Come in.'

When Emma put her head round the door, Mary's smile removed any doubts she might have had.

'Where's Mr Perfect?'

'Things aren't what they seem like…' Emma hastened to point out.

'Have you had dinner?'

'No.'

Emma followed Mary into the kitchen and waited till a delicious slice of cake and a coffee appeared in front of her. Her friend felt no resentment towards her, and was even trying to look after her by preparing something she knew she found tasty.

'So tell me. What's wrong? And don't tell me, "Nothing," because I shan't believe you.'

Emma began to talk. She didn't expect to find it so easy to describe things that sounded so wild and absurd, but Mary listened so attentively that the whole thing seemed normal, as if she were simply relating the adventures of some recent trip.

There was just one detail she omitted, something too intimate to share: Julian. She knew Mary was dying to know if she had a new relationship, but she was frightened to admit to something which she found hard to put into words.

She showed Mary the photocopies and the photo of the painting. The woman with the medieval headdress seemed to look at her with eyes astonishingly identical to her own. The curve of the cheeks, the broad forehead, the straight little nose, all looked familiar too.

'An amazing likeness,' Mary admitted. 'But such coincidences happen. What makes you think there's something uncanny about it? And what's it got to do with your hallucinations?'

'Right from the beginning I dreamed of a painting,' replied Emma, in a firm and convinced tone, 'a painting by an artist I'd never heard of before. My dreams have led me to find out more about this painter's biography. What you see here is the only painting of his that we know about. If it's a coincidence, it's the most stunning one you can imagine.'

Mary looked at her in bewilderment, as if her friend's words had been spoken in a foreign language and she needed all her concentration to understand them.

'There are two other people who've been experiencing the same symptoms as I have: Julian, and a boy of eighteen who can hardly believe what's happening to him. We feel ourselves drawn towards the museum as if a supernatural power were forcing us to go there.'

'I don't know what to say,' her friend replied. 'You're torturing yourself and suffering for something I can't comprehend. We still haven't figured out the explanation for your dreams, but now I see there's much more to it.'

'Yes, it's something that doesn't affect me alone. I want to carry on researching about this artist's life, and to discover the identity of that woman—'

'Let me talk to a couple of people. One possibility occurs to me: hypnosis.'

'Hypnosis?'

Emma was shocked. That sounded too drastic, too terrible. Something you see in films. She was frightened even to think of it.

She drained her coffee cup and was glad of the warming effect of the liquid on her body. Till that moment she hadn't noticed that her hands were freezing cold.

'There are studies of people who have discovered under hypnosis that they have a relationship with the past.'

'Do you mean they remember a previous life?'

'Something like that. I find it hard to credit, but it exists.'

Mary realised then that her friend was exhausted. Yet it was clear that Emma was grateful for the chance to talk to her. The conversation took them back to times they thought they had forgotten, times of friendship and trust between two young women with similar anxieties and the same desire to enjoy themselves.

'When I come out of work tomorrow, we can do something together. I'll see if I can help you. OK?'

Emma nodded, too tired to say more. If only, at least, she could rest during the night…

But she knew the dreams would return.

When she shut the door of her room, she put the photocopies on the table, making sure to leave the disturbing photo of the painting at the bottom of the pile. She didn't want to see it again. Not at that moment.

Like every night she organised her things for the next day: clean clothes, books, mobile. Her routine helped her maintain a certain degree of normality. But then she saw on the screen of her phone a notification of a missed call.

Maybe Julian, she thought.

But when she checked the number, she found it was the agency which had undertaken the search for her parents.

'Not now,' she said aloud, switching off the phone. She had more important things to think about.

5

THE GALLERY OF THE MUSEUM WAS MORE CROWDED than usual. Some schoolchildren were following their teacher's explanations without much interest, making jokes and comments as they moved from one picture to another. Outside it was a typical winter's day. There had even been a few flakes of snow driven by the wind, leaving a hint of white in some corners of the city.

Emma had been surprised to see Lucas there again. He looked paler and thinner, though he still kept his spectacular poster-boy look. He replied to Emma's silent question, telling her that the day before he had bought a ticket to London but had decided not to go.

'I wanted to talk to my family. To see my doctor. But in the end I couldn't face it. I had a horrible night. I just wanted to come here to ask you if you have an answer to all this.'

Emma sighed. No; no answer.

She was sitting next to Julian, as if seeking his protection from whatever might happen next, some future event which would sweep them on still further in their desperation. She longed to be alone with him, to tell him what she and Mary had discussed. But perhaps he wouldn't understand it. He didn't seem to approve of her effort to find an escape from their crisis. Withdrawn and resigned to persisting in his strange mental state, he seemed always so sure that there was nothing to be done.

Then they began to talk about their dreams and hallucinations. It was hard to distinguish their nightmares from real life, as if they belonged to both worlds simultaneously, a sensation that all three of them shared.

It was obvious that at the centre of their dreams lay the painting. They couldn't be sure what it represented: the figures in it dissolved into a landscape which they could barely make out. There were no faces. It was as if the three of them were lost in the middle of the image, trying to find a way out.

At the same time, an atmosphere of the past mingled with their nightmarish visions: streets, carriages, long dresses and top hats. Emma was the only one who could locate this environment precisely: it was the nineteenth century, the period whose artistic trends she was researching – without realising that one day they would become part of her life.

Alexander Robert Knight. He was the main focus of Emma's attention now: the man whose existence she had discovered through the dream. Something in his life must hold the key which would explain to them why his period and his work were appearing to them in this way.

Lucas still looked confused. He walked nervously up and down the gallery, paying attention to their conversation only intermittently, without giving the slightest credence to what to the others seemed obvious.

For a moment two female students looked at him in surprise, as if they had only just noticed him; they set about gazing at him with deliberately provocative smiles. He was evidently used to arousing the attention of women: he smiled back at them.

'I want to go to Ely.' Emma spoke so quietly that Julian had to lean towards her to hear her words. 'I want to look at the municipal archives. I want to find the documents from 1858. As we know, that's when Knight lived there. They might give us a lead.'

'Let me go with you,' Julian begged her. 'This time I want to go with you. If you're convinced about the idea, so am I. I want to get to the end of this story.'

Emma agreed, smiling broadly. She knew it would be a difficult journey, but with him everything would be different.

They decided to leave right away. Lucas didn't seem to bother very much what they did. He simply let himself be dragged along by these unconscious impulses without doing anything to avoid them. Nor did he understand this story which he had been half-listening to, about painters from the past who had no connection with what he himself was experiencing. If only he could go to London…

On the way to the station Emma tried to call Mary. This time she hadn't forgotten her friend. She owed her an explanation, and when she heard the automatic answer on the phone she left a message: 'I'll be away for the rest of the day. I don't know what time I'll be back, but I promise to keep in touch. Don't worry.'

*

The clouds had retreated and there had been no more snow. But it was very cold, even while the sun was still shining; and it was a pallid sun, dim and feeble.

Though the distance was very short, the train journey seemed interminable. Neither of them spoke, as if conserving their breath in anticipation of new events.

Emma recognised the Gothic cathedral from far off; it was one of the finest in the land. She tried to visualise what it would have looked like in the nineteenth century, when the first steam trains began to run in England. She couldn't tell whether it was the power of her imagination or a fresh hallucination, when she seemed to hear the unmistakable sound of a steam engine. The noise suddenly grew louder, beating rhythmically in her ears.

Equally suddenly the noise stopped, when the train, their real train, came to a halt. Julian helped her to step down, as if he realised what was happening in her brain.

'Do you think it was a good idea to come here?' he asked, when they were alone on the platform. She couldn't hide her anxiety: her cheeks were whiter, her hands shakier.

But yes; it was a good idea. Here was Alexander Knight's home. Here there might be an answer.

They went first to the tourist office, to get a plan of the city and some useful addresses.

Before graduating, Emma had already done some research on historical documents, archives and letters, so the practicalities weren't unfamiliar to her. Things were also easier because Ely was a small place, essentially built around the cathedral; there were no long distances to cover or huge offices to cope with. She made first for the small local library and the registry office.

In the library they were greeted by a cheerful-faced woman who seemed delighted to have something different to do instead of the usual monotony of her job. She wasn't unduly surprised by some questions which she had quite certainly never been asked before, and let Emma and Julian consult their store of newspapers from the nineteenth century.

It was there that they discovered a report of the death of Alexander Robert Knight in a tragic railway accident on the night of December 24, 1858. It seemed that his body had been found on the tracks, crushed by a train. The newspaper spoke of him with admiration; evidently he was a man whose loss had been mourned by the whole community. This grief, combined with the exceptional nature of the accident, had undoubtedly caused a great commotion in the town.

Impatience to discover more information was taking possession of both of them, as the figure of Knight grew ever more alive and more real. They were sure now that they were on the right path.

The archives of the registry office revealed details of births, including names of family members. The father, Robert Knight, had been a shopkeeper with a small fabric business in the town – a member of the working class who had achieved a degree of economic prosperity. There was a brother who lived in the north of England. At the time of Alexander's death his parents were no longer alive, so the inheritance passed to the brother. There were no other descendants.

There were some things which did not square with the image Emma had created in her mind. Obviously, as she now knew, Knight's career as a painter had been cut short. He had died young – at twenty-three, according to the date of birth recorded in the archive – but not from excess, by suicide, or as a consequence of the typical illnesses of the age, such as tuberculosis, but in an accident which even then had something peculiar about it. Crushed by a train on Christmas Eve. What a horrible way to die.

They also found the names of certain people who had some connection with him, having apparently either bought one of his paintings or engaged him as a portraitist.

How curious, Emma thought, that people from the upper class in that small community had had their portraits done by him. And where were those portraits now?

There were certain documents, signed by someone called Morgan, relating to payments for a number of paintings, and also a commission. But this time it wasn't a commission from an individual, but from the Fitzwilliam Museum in Cambridge. The document relating to the commission was dated 1858.

The Fitzwilliam. Now that *was* a revealing detail. Knight must have been working on a special painting, commissioned by none other than the Cambridge museum. But perhaps that work was never completed. There was no invoice or other document which might have confirmed delivery.

In any case it was the only clue which connected the painter with the Fitzwilliam – and which, through him, provided a link to themselves and their obsession with the museum. Could this be the key? The painting of their dreams, the painting which never reached its destination.

Julian didn't understand much of the process of reading documents written in a script which he found illegible. But it was fascinating to witness Emma's enthusiasm as she submerged herself in a period of English history which to him was so remote and foreign.

Hours passed. There were still many gaps in their knowledge of Knight's life, and they didn't know whether they would manage to fill them. Although the material was full of interest for Emma's thesis, their findings so far left unresolved the mystery which enveloped their own lives.

They were sitting side by side in a small room surrounded by shelves. The light was poor; it came from an antiquated fluorescent lamp above the table where they were reading. It was obvious that very few people came to this cold and unwelcoming room in the basement of the town hall. But Emma, engrossed in her research, seemed oblivious of her surroundings.

'You should take a break.' Julian interrupted her when he saw the tiredness in her eyes.

'We can't waste time,' she replied. When she looked back to the documents in front of her, she seemed to hear the sound of a distant train.

There *must* be something else. She was sure of it.

Who had modelled for him? Which painting was he was working on at the time of his death?

Emma now turned her attention to the name of the family which had bought some of his works. The Stevensons. It appeared they had lived first in South Africa, and then moved to Ely in – what a coincidence – 1858. So Knight had met them shortly before he died.

The couple had two daughters: Adelaide and Ariadne, born respectively in 1836 and 1840.

For a moment she imagined those young girls, perhaps overcome with excitement at having made the acquaintance of an artist.

It might be that they had modelled for one work or another, a family portrait, or even the Isolde painting. But that didn't explain the resemblance to Emma. Pure chance?

Nothing in the documents and invoices relating to Knight connected him with anyone who might have worked as his model. It could have been his girlfriend, or a lover… Nowhere was it mentioned that Alexander had been married, so there was no wife to pose for him. But

Emma well knew that artists used to find street women who would model for them, women without scruple who didn't mind exhibiting their body for a man. Some of the most famous artists of the period had painted in just that way. In that case the model might remain nameless. But who was the woman who so closely resembled her?

Emma smiled at Julian. She knew he was exhausted; bored, even. But he remained resolute, there at her side.

'We ought to find out if any correspondence survives between Alexander Knight and his clients or friends,' she commented. 'That would help us.' As she spoke the words, once more she thought she heard that distant train.

He nodded. In a way, that was something which related to his own work. He remembered his clients' letters and bills piling up on his desk. How he longed for things to go back to normal. But that would mean losing Emma…

Their eyes met once more.

Up on the first floor, in the office of one of the clerks, Emma obtained a new folder of documents. The man who had dealt with her handed it over with reluctance, probably keen to finish his day's work. But in view of what they had discovered already, Emma was sure that Knight had enjoyed a certain fame in the place where he lived. The fact that no historian seemed to have taken an interest in him might be because his works hadn't subsequently been considered of sufficient quality, or simply because most of them had been lost. Might they have been preserved by the descendants of those who had sat for portraits? But searching for them would be an impossible labour.

She carried on reading, her eyes clouded by sleepiness and by the dust from the folders. But then she found an envelope, containing what was certainly a letter. What she hadn't expected was that in that letter there appeared clearly the name of Dante Gabriel Rossetti.

She couldn't help uttering a cry of surprise, which alarmed Julian.

In the next group of papers she discovered another letter. And another. Some, dated "London, 1856", were about art classes, but there were two, dated "Ely, 1858", which looked more personal. The handwriting was difficult and the ink had already faded, but the contents showed that the two artists had remained friends.

Full of wonderment, Emma felt she was coming closer and closer to the lives of these men. She had read so much about the painters of the Brotherhood, and now she held in her hands a letter written by one of them, a letter which probably no one knew existed.

She imagined him as people had described him and as the surviving portraits depicted him: an ardent young man, rebellious, revolutionary in his time, filled with inspiration and with an idealistic and restless spirit which drove him to write poetry, to paint and to illustrate literary works.

Alexander Knight had undoubtedly learned from and worked with Rossetti, although at a certain moment in his life, two years later, he had left London for Ely. But the two had kept in contact by letter.

Why those letters were there, Emma didn't know. But they were surely objects of extraordinary value.

Rossetti must have known about his friend's death and about the painting, but nothing relating to that had come to light.

What fascinating lives, thought Emma, but how sadly they had ended. Knight crushed by a train in the flower of his youth, Rossetti some years later, after numerous bouts of depression, alone and semi-alcoholic. Yet upon one of them success and fame had smiled; for the other there was only oblivion. Perhaps Alexander's problem was that he had never been able to demonstrate his true merit. He didn't have time. Had things been different, the painting which he never finished would be hanging today in the Fitzwilliam.

As this thought entered her mind, Emma felt a strange uneasiness rise up within her. As if she were on the point of recalling something, without quite knowing what.

Alexander, she asked him mentally, what is happening to me? What connection is there between us?

6

At midnight she woke up screaming. She had heard the noise of the train again, and a feeling of terror had seized her. Everything was dark. Just that sound hammering in her ears. When she opened her eyes she seemed to hear the same sound dwindling into the distance. After that she hadn't wanted to sleep. She spent the time mentally rehearsing the previous day's discoveries.

Perhaps today's nightmares were due to exhaustion, mingled with intense emotion as a result of her visit to Ely with Julian. The life she had tried to track down had turned into an inexhaustible source of surprises. But at the same time, by forcing her mind to regress into the past, she had opened herself to images which became confused with real memories.

Now more than ever she felt the urge to return to the museum.

When they got back from Ely it was already late. Julian and Emma said their brief goodbyes. Mary was waiting for her. She noticed the feverish glint in Emma's eyes, and the heap of papers under her arm, but had no time for a long conversation. There would be time enough for that later.

The hours till dawn were unbearable for Emma, consumed as she was by impatience to discover more, but conscious too how difficult it would be to get all her questions answered.

Once more she went over the information she had uncovered, which was gradually giving shape to Alexander Knight's life. And, above all, to his death.

The discovery of his relationship with Rossetti confirmed what Emma had guessed already: that his style was similar to that of the Pre-Raphaelites. In those years he must also have known Edward Burne-Jones and William Morris. This finding would lend something important to her doctoral thesis, but it raised other questions too: in particular, why he had moved house instead of staying to work with those who were evidently his *maestri*. In any case, those letters didn't shed much new light, apart from some information about the work of the two artists. There were no confidences which might have revealed more personal details about Knight's life.

The names Morgan and Stevenson had been another trail to follow. Strangely there was no one currently living in Ely under either name. Even if there had been, though, they needn't necessarily have been descendants of those families from 1858.

At eight o'clock she called Julian. She wasn't surprised that he replied immediately. Presumably he hadn't been able to sleep either.

'Can we meet?' she asked him.

'Yes of course,' he replied, even though he knew the museum would still be closed.

'In half an hour, in the café on King's Parade.'

Before leaving, Emma put her head round Mary's door. She was reluctant to bother her as she knew she had to go to work, but she wanted to keep her up to date.

Mary responded with a smile. 'Don't worry. You know where to find me if you need me.'

Emma walked as if in a trance, still under the effects of the nightmare which had woken her. Try as she might, it was an effort to put her ideas in order.

Julian was waiting for her outside the café, in his unmistakable blue windcheater and his coloured scarf muffling him up to the nose. Emma had hardly given a thought to her appearance, so impatient had she been to leave the house. She had put on the first clean pullover that she came across, over some corduroy trousers and boots. They made her look like a first-year student.

They ordered extra-large coffees and currant muffins, then chose a table at the back, in search of warmth and a bit of privacy.

'Any news?' he asked.

Emma looked at him intensely. He seemed confused and preoccupied. That was natural, given the circumstances. Sometimes, when they were together and everything seemed to be going well, a pale ray of hope slipped into her heart. Yet Emma wasn't assured enough to take the first step. Julian appeared to be at ease with her, but for some reason didn't let things develop any further.

This was the moment for confidences. Away from home, away from the museum.

'No, no news,' she replied. 'I've been over what we read yesterday and it's all very interesting; but it doesn't clarify our situation. But I'm sure it has to do with this story: Alexander Knight, his death and the painting they commissioned.'

Julian stretched out his hand and rested it on her arm.

'What we discovered was fascinating,' Emma went on, 'but our minds are still functioning in a strange way.' Then she told him about her conversation with Mary the previous day – her suggestion about hypnosis.

'Can I ask you something more personal?' she said after a pause.

Julian hesitated, but only for an instant; he nodded and smiled. 'Of course.'

'Are you… gay?'

He burst out laughing, and the tension of the moment disappeared. 'Oh no! Is that the impression I give you?'

Emma laughed too, but nervously. She was frightened about where the conversation was leading her. All the same, she wanted to know.

'No, certainly not. But… you know…'

His expression changed. His gaze was deeper, harder.

'I was married many years ago, but it only lasted a few months. One fine day she left, and I had no more news of her. Later I found out that she'd given birth to a baby girl, and that nobody had told me anything. I didn't even know she was pregnant. For some time I searched for them, her and my daughter; but it came to nothing. It was very difficult to forget.'

'I'm sorry,' Emma managed to say. 'It must have been hard for you.'

'I know why you asked me that question. I see it constantly in your face: when we're in the museum, when we have a meal together… I know your feelings for me. I've got used to you, used to being with you, but I don't think this is the moment for a relationship. I'm very confused. When all this is over, we'll see. I need to settle some things first.'

Emma noticed him blushing. She drank a drop of coffee, trying to control her emotions.

He went on, 'And you? And… Paul?'

Paul? She barely remembered him. All that had gone away, along with other things in her life.

'He was my boyfriend for a while but, as I told you, we broke it off,' she answered.

'There's someone I've left behind in London,' said Julian pensively, more to himself than to the woman in front of him. 'Poor girl. She calls me every day and wants to come to join me here. She doesn't understand what's happening.'

He didn't understand it either. Somehow they needed to finish with all this and to restore order to their lives.

'Emma, you're an incredible person, intelligent and tenacious. I'd like to be with you. In spite of the age difference, we've got a lot in common. But I think it's better if we let things stay as they are for now. Over these last weeks I've been thinking that what's been happening to me is due to my emotional state, and that I've never properly moved on from an episode which is still affecting me, even if it happened long ago.'

Disappointment ran through Emma's body like a cold chill. Perhaps she had raised her hopes too high, perhaps she had misinterpreted this man who she had got to know in such strange circumstances. On the other hand, how easy was it for a man to say: 'You're a marvellous woman, but…'

She looked down at her watch to hide her confusion. Ten o'clock. The time had passed imperceptibly.

'Time for the museum,' she said.

'Yes. Our rendezvous. And today we know more than we did before.'

They got up and went out of the café. The wind in the street made them shiver.

As they walked, Julian looked at Emma with the sad expression which she knew so well.

'All these years,' he said suddenly, 'I've imagined what my daughter would be like. I've missed seeing her grow up, missed playing games with her, sharing moments with her, knowing if she's happy or unhappy. But I'll get over it. One day I'll be ready to form a family with someone new.'

'I understand,' Emma replied. She meant it, from the heart. She too had unfinished business from her past, something which was also affecting her now. But she said nothing.

When they entered the museum, the first person they saw was Lucas, sitting down, looking straight ahead of him as if he had seen a ghost. He didn't notice them until they spoke to him, as if waking him from a trance.

'I've seen it. I've seen the painting.' There was fear in his voice. 'It was here in front of me. And that face… It was me.'

He hid his face in his hands and began to weep like a child.

7

HOW SHE LET HERSELF BE PERSUADED, EMMA WAS STILL wondering. The first time Mary suggested it, it seemed a crazy idea. Therapy under hypnosis! Images came to her mind – from the television, or from some book – images of people who surrender their will to a supposed hypnotist and perform actions unconsciously, like puppets in a show designed to make the audience laugh.

Later, though, she took in the information which Mary gave her, and they discussed the matter. No, hypnosis wasn't a show which played with a person's actions and made them lose control of their body. Rather, it was a modern therapy which was achieving surprising success in curing some kinds of sleep disorder and other mental and emotional problems. It has been proved that, in situations of extreme stress, hypnosis produces excellent results in those kinds of patients.

Emma tried to recall all this as she went that morning to her appointment at a clinic on the outskirts of

London. Mary's contacts in the world of psychiatry and psychology had assured her that this was an absolutely trustworthy establishment. Even so…

After waiting for a few minutes Emma was met by a blonde and elegant nurse in a clean, well-lit room decorated in a style quite unlike that of a hospital.

'There's no need to be nervous,' she said with a smile, as she led Emma along corridors painted white to the ceiling, with a series of glass doors leading off them. Soft music in the background reinforced the impression of a setting designed for the complete relaxation of body and spirit.

Mary had made her excuses at work so that she could accompany Emma. She owed it to her. She knew how much Emma was suffering, how great was the anxiety that tormented her, and she tried to help her as best she could, longing for her to be free of the ghosts that overwhelmed her and prevented her from living. Beside her was Julian, worried and nervy, trying to simulate a tranquillity that he did not feel, disguising the jumble of emotions inside him: unease at being present at an exceptional and intimate occasion; fear; doubt. After all, this matter affected him too. He himself might be undergoing the same treatment, attempting to probe what lay concealed in the depths of his brain. And, on the other hand, today he wasn't at the museum. He felt the lack as if he were failing in an inescapable duty.

Emma now found herself in another room, as clean and white as the previous one, with subdued lighting and an aroma which she recognised as lavender. Nothing strange, nothing intimidating, nothing to make her feel uncomfortable. On the contrary, it was like the bedroom of a luxury hotel, designed in accordance with the latest fashions in decoration. The relaxation couch she lay down on reminded her of a holiday she had once had in France, when she went to a spa for a massage. That brief, distant memory gave her a little of the security that she needed.

A young man came up to her, shook her hand and explained the procedure. Above all she must have confidence in what was happening and be totally relaxed. There were some people whose unconscious rejected hypnosis; in these cases nothing could be done. When he asked her for her personal details, she explained her family situation and the fact that she had been an adopted daughter who had never known her real parents. But that was a different matter. Something more urgent had brought her there. She told him about her visions, her anxiety, and the dreams.

When the man began the session, she was ready. She fixed her eyes on the man's hand. In a little while her heart began to beat faster and her breath became rapid and irregular. She was suffocating.

She felt as if she were sliding down, as if she were on a toboggan, dragged along to some unknown place at the bottom. Her body shook violently.

'Don't resist,' she said to herself. 'Let yourself go.'

From that moment on she abandoned herself to what the man was doing with her: his hands, his voice. She had nothing to lose. And for the first time for ages she had the sensation that her muscles were relaxing and that the tension was disappearing. Little by little, a complete peace was invading her.

Then the images began to take shape in her mind. At first there were individual scenes, like those in a dream, vague and insubstantial. Then they began to take on meaning, to become real. The time was passing…

The voice of the hypnotist reached her ears, distant, distorted, as if it had to cross an immense space filled with cotton wool.

'Where are you now?'

'In an artist's studio,' she replied immediately, without hesitation.

There were many paintings all around her; on some the canvas was still empty; others were already finished. A young man with curly brown hair and a short beard was preparing colours on a palette. When his eyes turned towards her, such was the intensity of his gaze that it seemed to pass right through her.

The style of the room was unmistakable: the armchair, the high ceiling, the fireplace, the ornaments. There could be no doubt about the era in which she found herself.

'The year is 1858,' she said.

'And who are you?'

'The woman in the painting.'

She couldn't tell how she realised this. It came as a revelation, or rather as an inexplicable sensation.

The artist was working on a canvas on which the details were still imperceptible. There was a landscape with flowers and rich vegetation, also some figures whose faces were unfinished. Her studies in the history of art led her immediately to identify the colour, the manner, the painterly idiom of the artists of the time.

'What does the painting represent?' said a voice.

'An ancient myth, the story of Venus and Adonis. The goddess Venus fell in love with a beautiful young man who had been born from the incestuous union between a father and his daughter. As a punishment, the daughter was turned into a tree.'

Then she noticed that there were two other people with her: a man of middle age, and another much younger man, almost an adolescent. The older man bore an extraordinary resemblance to Julian. Maybe he was older than Julian, though that might just have been the impression created by the formal, dark clothes he was wearing. She took longer to recognise the youth. Was it Lucas? But he seemed no more than a child…

The two of them were also posing for the painting.

The painter laughed and made jokes. She was surely flirting with the three of them, though later, at a certain moment, she heard herself saying the word "papa".

'Are there any other people there with you?'

'Yes.'

'Who are they?'

'Two men. One of them is my father.'

Then everything became dark. When she once more became aware of her surroundings, she found that she was no longer inside a room, but in the open air, at night. She was walking down a deserted, badly lit street.

Again the voice reached her, like a distant echo.

'Where are you now?'

'In a railway station. But it is very dark. And I am frightened.'

Yes, she was frightened. She sensed that someone was following her, but she couldn't say who or why. Just a faceless shadow.

'Do you know what you're doing here?'

'I am meeting someone.'

How strange! She didn't know why, just that it was important.

'I have to save Alexander.' The words flowed from her of their own accord. 'He's in danger.'

Then she heard it. A train coming towards her with a sound like thunder, approaching nearer and nearer.

At the same time she saw two people walking next to the railway tracks. One she recognised immediately; it was the same man she had seen in the studio: the painter. In spite of the hat and overcoat which covered him almost completely, there was no mistaking his appearance and the way he walked. The other man was moving stealthily, as if trying to avoid being seen, taking advantage of the darkest corners to blend with the night itself. Black upon black.

It all happened in an instant, as if in one of those nightmares where scenes flash past so rapidly that they can barely be seized or memorised. The train was almost upon them when the second man pushed the first violently onto the tracks. She heard a cry above the noise of the engine, and saw them struggling; finally the train swept past in front of her, covering her in smoke and blinding her vision.

Shivering with cold and terror she ran to the station, huddling in a corner. The tears sprang uncontrollably and poured down her cheeks. What could she do? She knew he was close by, dead, his shattered body lying on the tracks. Now all she could do was to weep for him.

But there was someone else there, someone who could hear her sobbing in the silence which followed the passing of the train. The murderer.

Of his identity there could be no doubt: her own father. At that moment she knew she could not return home. She had to flee – anywhere! – to escape from him. At last she understood what had happened. What a fool she had been! For her it had been a game: her love for Alexander, and her other love, so special, for her darling father. In a way she was like the girl in the myth. Father and lover had coalesced into one individual. And she, in her innocence, had believed she could satisfy two men, while both of them were consuming themselves with passion and jealousy. The difference was that whereas the feelings of the one were authentic and honest, those of the other were cruel and perverted. Feelings which had gone so far as to lead her to cause a death.

She watched him leave. The station remained in silence. The rain had stopped.

She would need to conserve all her strength to survive, to keep the child whom she carried in her womb. Alexander would no longer be there to protect her. And there would be no one to finish the painting.

'Do you know now what it was that you wanted to tell him?'

'That I was expecting his child.'

'And who was that woman?'

'Ariadne.'

Little by little, Emma felt her breathing return to normal. The beating of her heart was more measured. In her mind the image of the station became ever more faint, until it disappeared altogether.

When she woke up she was still on the couch. The hypnotist was looking at her with an expression of satisfaction and perplexity.

Emma replied as best she could to his questions, recalling what she had seen, without being sure whether it had simply been a dream – albeit a very realistic one – but nothing more than that.

'The experience you have lived through was quite extraordinary. Few people manage to achieve anything like it. Some investigators think that cases like this demonstrate a person's recollection of a previous life – though to me that's questionable.'

She didn't know what to say. Yet suddenly she was conscious that something very unusual had happened – that a transformation had taken place within her. Now the pieces fitted together. Now she knew. However astonishing it might seem, now she was sure that everything she had experienced was true, and that it explained her nightmares, her anxiety and her visits to the museum, driven by a force more potent than her own will.

The painting had never been in the Fitzwilliam, because Alexander had never had the chance to complete it. And they were a part of the painting.

Smiling timidly, Emma said goodbye to the people who had attended her during the session, and went out of the room, leaving behind that other world which she had briefly inhabited, to rejoin now her own present, the time to which she belonged.

Outside, Mary and Julian were waiting for her impatiently. When they saw her, their expressions suggested that they had seen a ghost. And that was what she resembled: a spectre who has just returned across the threshold of the kingdom of the dead.

For a moment all were silent: they, unable to think what to ask her; she, uncertain where to begin her story.

'It's over now,' she said at last. 'And I'm OK. But let's get out of here.'

They walked a short distance to the bus stop: two young women and an older man. Were it not for their tense and worried expressions, they might have been three friends or workmates going out for a meal.

The bus took them to the centre of London. None of them was in a hurry to catch the train. For now, nothing demanded their presence in Cambridge.

To avoid attracting attention they chose a small café where most of the customers were tourists – is there *anywhere* in London where there are no tourists? The salads and fresh sandwiches on the counter looked appetising.

Emma felt as if she were gradually recuperating, returning to normal life, as if she had just woken after a long sleep. The smells and tastes seemed different to her.

The other two waited anxiously for an explanation which didn't come. Yet just by looking at Emma they could tell that the session had been a success, and that the change they had been longing to find in her had taken place.

Suddenly, abruptly, she spoke. 'Alexander Knight didn't commit suicide. He was murdered because he fell in love with his model and was going to marry her. Her father wanted to prevent it. We were the characters in the unfinished painting. In our hallucinations we were recreating the era in which our lives had been frozen into immobility at the moment of Alexander's death. Our experiences were those of the models for the painting, and at the same time the experiences of the figures we were going to represent, like actors in the theatre.'

She continued talking, heedless of the astonished eyes staring at her across the table. With every word, her transformation seemed more and more complete.

'In my thesis I'll provide all the information about Alexander's death. I owe it to him. He might have become a great artist, but a man murdered him in cold blood and escaped punishment. His crime never came to light.'

Emma told them how she had felt when she witnessed the events at the station with her own eyes – or rather, with the eyes of her mind. Her pain was the pain which that woman, Ariadne, had suffered as she watched the death of the man she loved.

In confusion, Julian asked her, 'And who was I in all this?'

'You too were in the painting. You were the father.'

Mary couldn't believe what she was hearing. It went far beyond anything she could have imagined. For some time Emma had assumed the personality of this Ariadne, a girl who had posed for a painting in 1858.

'I know what the subject of the painting was,' Emma continued. 'The plot of that ancient myth almost becomes reality.'

'And Lucas? Why did he have the same sensations as us?'

'He was Adonis. There was a boy there, a very special boy, very good-looking, who was going to lend his appearance to the mythical character who was loved by a goddess and died a tragic death. I don't know if that sounds familiar to you…'

Julian and Mary nodded. Adonis. The embodiment of male beauty.

'We have to call Lucas now,' said Mary. 'He too deserves to know this.'

'There's something else,' Emma added. 'Now we know the true identity of the model for the painting, I've been thinking that it's possible Ariadne was my ancestress. Hence the resemblance. They had a child: the child Alexander never knew.'

Julian hesitated. 'I'm still not sure I believe it, but maybe you're right.'

Three characters from a painting, impelled towards the museum to which they would have belonged, trying to solve the mystery of the death of the artist who would have immortalised them. And in 1858, four people embroiled in a sordid story which had remained hidden for more than a century.

Was it Alexander who had guided them back to his own time to uncover the crime?

It sounded crazy. But now, none of them had any doubt about its truth.

8

EMMA HAD SPENT THE MORNING ORGANISING HER BOOKS and the papers relating to her thesis. For a while she listened to music, then got down to work.

Only four days had passed since the hypnosis session, but it already seemed like an eternity.

Things had gradually returned to normal. She knew Julian was preparing to go back to London. Soon they would part.

One day they saw Lucas. He was with a girl and looked pleased with himself. When they told him everything that had happened, he reacted with the expected astonishment and incredulity, but listened attentively to their extraordinary story. Whether he attributed the mysterious ending of his sickness to Emma's discoveries, they couldn't say. In any case, his symptoms had gone away as inexplicably as they had first arrived. That seemed to be enough for him.

Emma went back once more to London, this time to visit the agency which was handling the enquiry into her parents' identity. Over the last few days she had completely forgotten the repeated calls logged on her mobile. But finally she had made contact with them, in a mood of surprise and anticipation.

Their response had been positive: they had some news.

Was it possible they had finally found someone? Would she know her real parents? What a capricious destiny that this should occur precisely when so many other things had been happening in such a relentless sequence!

The person she spoke to in London mentioned various possibilities which they had been considering, and assured her that they would have an answer soon. Before long they would post the relevant documentation to her, along with the papers which Emma had originally handed over to them to initiate the enquiry.

So there was nothing to do but wait. Again. She was used to it.

*

When Mary came back home, it was lunchtime. Emma couldn't contain herself and rushed out excitedly to meet her. When she saw her, Mary feared the worst: in spite of everything, the nightmares and hallucinations must have returned.

'What's wrong?' she dared to ask, as if reluctant to hear the answer. 'Again? The museum, the dreams…?'

'No, no,' Emma laughed, 'the next time I go to the museum it will be because I really want to, when there's an interesting new exhibition to see. No, it's about my parents—'

'Your parents?'

Mary was genuinely amazed now. She had never put much faith in this search by Emma for her real parents. Sometimes she had even thought that Emma was making a mistake, that the fact of discovering the identity of her biological parents was entirely unimportant. Emma *had* her parents, "real" or not.

'Yes. During the hypnosis session I thought I might remember something about my real family, something that might help me locate my past. But nothing came of it. But now I think the agency has found some information. Maybe one day I might get to know my true parents.'

Emma smiled like a child promised a visit to Disneyland. A new hope, added to the inner sense of liberation which she had recently experienced. Something to banish the sadness which had gripped her when she had to accept that her feelings for Julian were not reciprocated.

'Are you sure it's what you want?' Mary asked hesitantly.

'What do you mean?'

'Well, I know it's important to you, but… I don't know, maybe you should think again. It might be hard. It could make you resent them for abandoning you.'

Mary's words didn't dampen Emma's enthusiasm.

'There speaks the psychologist!' she laughed. 'Don't worry. I'm sure it will all turn out for the best, and that when it's over I'll be able to carry on with my life.'

In fact it seemed like a sign to face the future with optimism. It didn't matter whether her father turned out to be a convict or a wealthy businessman, her mother a housewife, a journalist or a prostitute. Nor did she see it as disloyal to Anna Carter, the woman who had brought her up; all she knew was that, when the solution was found, she could be at peace.

The documents arrived that same afternoon. They were in a bulky white envelope, with the name of the agency in one corner.

Mary had already gone to her classes, and her other two flatmates wouldn't be back till evening. Emma was glad she could enjoy absolute privacy. She was so nervous that she almost forgot the events that had been happening until just a few days ago.

She opened the envelope and carefully examined the papers inside, one by one: a birth certificate, the results of some DNA tests, a certificate from a registry and a name: Linda Clarence, deceased two years previously. Her married name had been White, the wife of Ewan Julian White. In 1984 she gave away for adoption a baby girl, recently born in a small village in Somerset. It seemed that the family which adopted the child never knew the mother personally. They moved to London, where any possibility of contacting the biological mother lapsed. She and the father had already separated when the child was born, and Linda alleged that her husband had abandoned her.

Emma had to read this several times in order to assimilate it. Impossible. It couldn't be true. Madness. Nonsense.

Her first thought was to call the agency to tell them they'd made a mistake.

Once again she looked at the documents, on which the letters seemed to be dancing, mingling one with another and jumbling up the names. But in the end she had to admit that it was clear: the agency she had paid to find her real family had discovered that Julian White was her father.

She spent more than an hour wholly absorbed, her mind a blank, unable to decide what to do. She wanted to cry but couldn't. She wanted to laugh but couldn't.

At last she made a decision. She picked up her mobile and keyed in Julian's number, mentally praying that he wouldn't reply.

But he answered immediately.

'Emma, hi. How are you?'

'I need you to come here and see something. Please. Now.'

She didn't have the strength to explain.

He hesitated. Her voice sounded so different… 'Has something happened?'

'Please.'

'All right. I'll be at your house as soon as I can.'

As with Mary, Julian's first reaction had been one of fear. They both thought everything had been sorted out – but maybe they were wrong.

Full of apprehension, he made for Emma's house, uncertain what he would find there. He was worried that she had been upset by their conversation a few days earlier; but it was better to have been honest with each other. He hoped she understood that. And yet in a way he still missed the moments they had shared when they sat side by side in the museum, like two beings who belong to another world.

When she greeted him, her expression was strange, as if she were afraid. But what was she afraid of now?

Before he had time to say anything, she handed him some papers.

'What's this?' he asked.

'I already told you that I too had some unfinished business with my past,' she replied, her eyes lowered to avoid his enquiring look. 'This is what I found out.'

He began to read. While he did so, Emma observed him. Now she realised why Julian had always seemed familiar to her, as if she had known him before: they resembled each other. The hair, the shape of the jaw, the nose, the lips…

When he raised his eyes, they were filled with tears. 'Emma… I…'

'I'm sorry, I'm sorry,' she answered, in a very gentle voice. And he understood what she meant. She was sorry to have hoped for a relationship with him, sorry her heart had been full of him, to love him as a woman loves a man, a partner, a lover, not a father.

'You've nothing to be sorry about. You didn't know.'

Julian went close to her and opened his arms. He had always wanted to protect her. Was it because he had an unconscious intuition of the truth?

Emma let him embrace her, resting her head on the chest of this man who until recently had been unknown to her, and who now turned out to be her true father. And she started to weep. So many tears were stored inside her, so many emotions which now poured out.

'Do you know how often I've longed to be able to embrace my daughter? You can't imagine it.'

Emma stopped crying, still embarrassed. It hadn't been her fault. She had been like a female version of Oedipus, destined to discover her real father in the man she loved, though in their own case nothing more had happened between them. She felt no guilt about her feelings and longings. Sometimes love is born without asking permission, regardless of age, social barriers or other impediments. It belongs to human nature.

Julian gazed at her in admiration. How young Linda and he had been when they got married! Almost children. Emma was now already a fully-fledged woman who had gone to university and was about to get her doctorate. He contemplated the contours of her face, her blonde hair falling to her shoulders, her slim figure, and noticed the little details that the two of them had in common.

When Emma spoke again, her voice was firmer, more confident. It was better not to recall the moments when she had longed to feel the softness of his lips against hers...

'Do you see? Everything that has happened to us – the nightmares, the visions, the anxiety, the theme of the painting – it all hinges on a story about an unusual relationship between a father and his daughter. It's as if we've acted out that story, as if it happened precisely to *us* because we were father and daughter.'

'What do you mean?'

'The story of Adonis. He was born from an incestuous union between a father and a daughter. And then… Ariadne was the object of an unnatural passion on the part of her own father.'

Julian shuddered. Perhaps she was right, that there was a connection between the incredible events of recent weeks and the relationship between himself and Emma. A mysterious coincidence. As mysterious as all the rest.

'Alexander was the victim of the passion which a father felt for his daughter,' Emma added pensively.

Julian couldn't take his eyes off her. But his own feelings had been quite clear. There had been no ambiguity about them. Or had there?

'Emma, I hope you'll visit me one day, and we can gradually come to have a normal relationship. I'm sure you'll like my gallery. In a way you've followed family tradition by studying art history, don't you think? And on the day you have your doctoral *viva*, be sure I'll be there.'

'OK… Dad?' She laughed. 'I don't think I'll ever get used to calling you "Dad". For me you'll always be Julian.'

Suddenly they heard the door of the flat opening. Mary had come back. Emma felt herself trembling. What would Mary think when she found the two of them still together?

When she saw Emma's door open and Emma sitting very close to Julian, Mary couldn't hide her surprise. Her first thought was that at last her friend was enjoying herself a bit, and she didn't want to spoil her fun.

Mary was already tiptoeing her way to her own room when Emma called her back.

'Mary, can I introduce you properly? This is Julian White. My father.'